SASQUATCH PRISON DIARY

HIDDEN MOUNTAIN CHRONICLES
BOOK 2

PATRICK TALMADGE

HANGAR 1 PUBLISHING

1

My name is Matt Hurley. I am an elite runner training in the Cascade Mountains of Washington State. Two years ago, I was looking for the perfect training course for an ultra-race when I found a diary. This story is about a diary I found and everything that happened to me after finding it.

Scoping out trails in the mountains, I found a logging road that had closed due to a bridge washout caused by a heavy rainstorm in the spring. The economy was in the tank back then, and fixing the bridge wasn't in the state's budget. That meant I hoped that I would have this road all to myself for years, with no cars flying around corners endangering me. Because the river was too wide and deep to cross without a bridge, no noisy dirt bikes would be making dust trails and bothering me. The only noise and dust would be from my running shoes, making little puffs of sound and dirt as I ran. It might be years until the state could afford to fix the bridge, and I was not at all sorry to have it all to myself.

As with long-distance running, finding a safe place to train is tough. Across the river, I'd have my own running loop in the mountains all to myself. Perfect. I could concentrate on training, and if I got tired or hurt, I would only have to run or walk halfway around in either direction before I reached my camp. I preferred the area near the top of my loop because it was quiet and cooler in the late summer months. It took me longer to get to camp, but I was here for weeks at a time and peace was what I craved most.

It was an ideal situation, and I had it all to myself.

I used a raft to cross the river, then moved my gear on a cart to my base camp. To get across the 100-foot distance, I found a slow spot in the river upstream and out of sight of the bridge that would allow me to get my raft safely across. Tying a safety rope to a tree on one side, then to the other, enabled me to cross without worry of being washed downstream in the event of an accident. No paddling, I just pulled myself across. This was handy during spring run-off when the snow melts, the water is high and it can be dangerous.

I had been in the mountains for six days doing loops on my empty road when I felt a slight tightness in my right leg. When you run ultras, you must listen closely to your body, because if something physically starts going wrong, and you run another ten or twenty miles, you can really injure yourself. If injured, I could be out for weeks or months.

Being a smart runner, I slowed to a walk so I could feel what was happening. I walked for a couple minutes, and it was still feeling tight. I sat on a log at the base of a cliff in the shade while I massaged my leg and rested. It is common for top runners to walk, so I was not wimping out by stopping.

It was a warm July morning, and the cool shade felt good. I had been training hard for years and knew a day or two off would not affect my fitness. Some runners make a mistake by training too many days, so they never really recover. I would take at least two days a week off and sometimes three.

The leg did not seem to be loosening up quickly, which meant a rest stop. I took my hydration pack off, pulled out my emergency blanket, walked over to a small patch of grass and spread out my blanket so I could lie down in the grass in comfort. After five minutes, a bit of color above on the side of the cliff caught my eye. It was yellow and looked like part of a flag. I could not really tell what it was, but I was curious, so I got up to have a closer look.

I am one of those people who stops to investigate every bag or piece of trash to see if it is worth anything. I had never found much, but sometimes, while on a long, dreamy run, I'd fantasize about finding a bank bag full of money.

I walked over to the base of the cliff, and once I was standing right under it, I could tell it was a backpack. Now I was really curious. I really wanted to know what was in the pack. I had already decided to stop running because of the tight leg and would be walking back to my camp, so I was not missing any training by taking the time to look closer. The cliff looked a bit steep to climb without the proper gear, so I looked for a way to the top through the brush further up the road.

About 200 feet away, I saw a promising game trail and turned uphill toward what I hoped was a spot above the pack. I marked the spot directly above the pack by picking a weird-shaped huge tree above where the pack was hanging. The game trail kept going up and intersected a much larger trail near the top. This new trail was smooth and wide and went both left and right and looked more like a dirt road than a game trail. I could still see the weird-shaped tree above the pack to my left and headed that way. Making my way to the cliff edge below the tree, I held my breath and looked over the edge. Fifteen feet below me was the pack. Now how was I going to retrieve it?

Looking closer, I saw a thick tan twine wrapped around the pack. Directly above the pack, I saw someone had tied one end of the thick twine to a bush at the edge of the cliff and dropped the pack over the edge. I pulled on the twine, and the pack came with it. I smiled in anticipation of what I would find but hoped it was nothing gross like a head or something.

The pack was heavy for such a small daypack, making me even more eager to check it out. After untying the rope and unzipping the pack, I peeked in. Being careful not to breathe in, in case it was something toxic, I detected a slightly musty odor and saw a thick plastic bag covering something square like a notebook. Underneath the first plastic bag was a second bag, and inside this one was a heavy old leather bag. When I squeezed the bag, it felt like a bunch of heavy metal disks. Nothing else was in the pack. OK, now I was really letting my imagination go wild. *This is it, Matt,* I thought, *you finally hit pay dirt.* I wanted to save the heavy bag for last to keep my dream of riches going just a bit longer before reality dashed it like all the other times when I had found something. So, I started with the plastic bag with what felt like a notebook.

The notebook definitely looked old and looked like a sketchbook or scrapbook. Inside, it was apparent it was a handwritten diary. There were three loose pages slipped into the front of the notebook. Someone named Doug had written a few hurried words.

There was an accident. I am being kidnapped. If you find this, please try to find me. Use these gold coins to help find me. There are thousands more for whoever does.

I read the words "thousands more", dropped the notebook, and quickly tore into the heavy leather bag. Sure enough, there were coins that looked and felt like gold. I hollered, then looked around, although I knew I was alone. I poured the coins out onto the plastic bag the book came in and picked two up, looking closely at them. They all looked old but in great shape. Some of the coins were US $20 gold coins, and most were from the 1800s. Other coins were foreign and looked weird, but they were heavy, like the US gold coins, and appeared genuine. Laying the coins out on top of the bag, I began to count. "Ninety-eight, ninety-nine—one hundred!" There were 100 of the $20 US gold coins and over another 100 of the foreign coins.

I knew they were valuable but had no idea what they were worth. I had collected a few coins myself but could never afford gold. But I knew who could help me determine their value, thinking of the coin shop I usually visited. It felt like the weight of the coins in the bag was at least ten pounds. I pumped my fist in the air and gave another whoop. If these coins were real, I was going to be rich!

Putting the coins back into the leather bag, I pulled the loose pages out and continued to read.

The next words said, "I got hurt while hiking, then got rescued. But they won't let me go."

After I finished reading the loose pages, I had to stop and think for a while.

The date on the loose pages meant Doug was "rescued" six years earlier. He dropped the pack over the cliff three years ago, just after the bridge washout. If this was real, that meant this guy named Doug had been captive for six years.

It was no wonder no one had found the pack until I did. Doug must have seen the road below the cliff and thought a passerby might see the pack hanging there and rescue him. He didn't know the road would soon be closed because of the bridge washout. If I hadn't stopped to massage my leg, I never would have seen it either. Leaves and dirt had mostly covered the pack over the last three years. It was just lucky I had seen a patch of yellow that had remained uncovered.

And lucky for me, there were gold coins in the bag. When I read what Doug wrote next, I would have dismissed this as a hoax if it hadn't been for the coins. In fact, I snorted out loud when I read the next line.

I have been captured by a group of Sasquatches. To prove this, inside the bag, there is hair from five different individuals. Please contact my mother, my only living relative. I want her to know I am alive.

I looked in the bag again, and in a bit of carefully wrapped plastic flattened between the diary's pages, there were some coarse dark hairs. OK, now this was getting really interesting. Either this guy Doug was nuts, or there was a camera taking my picture for a TV show, or this was real. But the coins seemed so real. And Doug gave his mother's address in Seattle, not far from the area where I lived.

The last of the loose pages were maps that showed where he had traveled with the Sasquatches and approximately where they were at certain times of the year. And then Doug wrote: "They pass this spot every few weeks during May through September."

Startled, I looked around at the well-traveled trail nearby. It was now July. If this was real, I needed to do something quickly because there were only two months left of their traveling season through this area. But did I really want to get involved? The thought of Sasquatches holding this guy was scary. I didn't really believe it, but I thought I'd read the rest of the diary to make up my mind and figure out if it was for real.

It was now 9:00 in the morning, and I still needed to rest my leg a bit longer before walking back to camp, so I picked a dry spot next to the weird, crooked tree to sit and read.

Once I started reading Doug's diary, I could not stop. After an hour of reading, I started getting nervous. Every time I heard the slightest rustling in the bushes, I startled and looked around, expecting to see a Sasquatch. I had run in the woods alone for years and had never been scared or worried before. Now here I was reading a stupid diary I found and was spooked. I couldn't keep my eyes on the pages because I kept looking over my shoulder for big hairy men, so I packed up the diary, grabbed the backpack and started heading back to my camp.

It was noon by the time I returned to my camp, and I was starved. A quickly fixed a sandwich, and a beer, and I began to feel comfortable enough to start reading again. After reading for another stretch, I really had the willies. I was miles away from the trail Doug said the Sasquatch traveled on, but I now did not feel safe in any part of the Cascade Mountains.

It was 3:30 in the afternoon and much too late to break camp and make it the twelve miles back to my van before dark. But after reading the diary, I didn't think I'd be comfortable hiking at night ever again. I was thoroughly spooked and didn't want to sleep on the ground.

Doug had written that Sasquatch could not climb, which is why he had tied his backpack off and thrown it over the cliff. With that in mind, I climbed up a large tree and set up my climbing hammock between two trees about thirty feet above the ground. I always carried my tree hammock in case I ended up in bear country and didn't feel safe sleeping on the ground. No matter where I am, I always keep my food cache high up in a tree so animals, especially bears, can't get at it.

After eating dinner, I climbed back up the tree, slipped into my sleeping bag, and then secured my climbing harness to the tree hammock's loops. Most people don't use safety straps when zipped into a secure setup like this, but I don't ever take chances. Yah, I'm the guy that always wears a helmet when biking. I hoisted the rest of my gear by rope and settled in for the night.

It was too early to go to sleep, so I put on my headlamp and read more of the diary, finally finishing it late into the night. That book took me hours longer to read than normal as I kept going over and over the same sentences. I just could not believe what I was reading.

I knew I would not be able to sleep because I felt more scared than I had ever been in my life. The coins seemed real enough because they were so heavy, and I could see and touch them. But the part about there being Sasquatches in the story made it hard to swallow. Being alone in the deep forest for six days and nights was a perfect formula for my uneasiness and fear. At about three a.m., I was still unable to sleep, although secure in my tree nest. No way I was staying any longer. I'd head back home first thing in the morning and skip the rest of my month-long training trip.

While I felt scared, I was totally intrigued by the diary and wanted to find out if it was for real. I did sleep that night in fits and snatches, but when I lay awake, I thought about what I had read and tried to imagine what it was like to live as a prisoner of the Sasquatch.

2

The next morning after the most fitful night I had ever experienced, I packed my gear, which now included a heavy backpack of coins and the diary, and started hiking, making it out to my van in record time. I felt creeped out all the way to the river and kept looking over my shoulder as I hiked. Twice I almost wet myself when I heard a noise. One of those times, I spooked a deer which made a loud noise as it burst through the brush, trying to get away from me. My startled yell echoed through the forest as the deer scrambled away from me. That was the first time since finding the pack that I managed a smile.

Every time I passed a game trail, I looked in both directions to make sure there were no Sasquatches lurking in the shadows. I couldn't remember a time in the woods when I felt so on edge and scared of every noise. Normally on a hike or run, I'd enjoy the sounds of small animals when I encountered them. This time I jumped at each sound. I had fantasies of finding the Sasquatch sitting around my van when I got there, and I couldn't get out of those woods fast enough to suit me.

Once I reached the river, I held onto my safety rope, got myself across, and hurried to get myself and gear to the van as soon as possible. I tossed my gear into the back of the van and sighed in relief as I locked the vehicle's door. In a hurry to get home, I drove straight to Seattle, not even stopping at my favorite hamburger place on the way back.

The value of the coins was on my mind as I unloaded, dropping my gear on the floor right inside the door, which is not something I usually do. Then I quickly fired up my laptop and looked up the value of similar gold coins. It seemed wise to get an idea of what the coins were worth before heading to the coin dealer I knew. I wanted to be ready for negotiations, if necessary, and knowing approximate prices would be helpful. At the back of my mind was Doug's plea on the loose pages to contact his mother. But first, I'd check out the coins.

Was any of this real?

If the coins were real, and this guy's story checked out, I knew I was in for a real ride with the press if I said anything. Should I call the police? If I contacted them, would I be able to get any more coins or keep the ones I already had? I know it sounds cheap and self-serving, but I wasn't rich. This might be my shot. I wanted to make sure I could get something out of it and still help this Doug guy if he was for real.

I looked up the US $20 gold coins first, and my jaw dropped. I might even have drooled a little, my mouth was open so far. The dates I checked said they were worth from $1,300 to $3,500. The best coins were worth $5,000 to $15,000—*each*. And these were in near-perfect condition. OK, now I was starting to feel my head swim. I laid the coins out by dates and mint marks, then compared them to the list.

When I found at least six of the coins were rare, I started to sweat. Three were worth over $50,000 to $100,000. But the last three coins made the whole thing almost blow my mind. Two were worth over $400,000, and one was worth almost a million. There were only six of the one coin known to exist, so its price was extra high.

I sat for a while and thought. I had over two million dollars worth of coins already, and I had not checked the other hundred coins.

It took hours of searching to determine what half the foreign

coins were and their value. After another couple of hours of searching, I figured out the other half of the coins were Spanish
doubloons. The average value of a Spanish doubloon was around
$4,000 each for a decent-shaped one, and mine were perfect. That
meant I must have another five hundred thousand to a million
dollars worth of coins. If I really had two to three million dollars in
gold, I would not have to work another day in my life. And if I
looked for and actually found Doug, I could buy my own island or
anything else I wanted.

But were they real? I had to go to my coin dealer and see if these
coins were real and what he thought they were worth. I quickly
placed each coin into a separate small plastic bag. Then I put each
coin with the same mint date into a larger bag.

With the coins placed in one of my backpacks, along with the
diary, I headed to the coin shop, holding the backpack close and
thinking about what I would tell Randy.

Randy was in his early forties and had dealt with coins since he
was young. He had worked with his dad in the business, then took it
over when his dad unexpectedly passed away. I had known him for
almost ten years, met him playing racquetball, and always felt I could
trust him. I figured the best thing would be to tell him the truth.
Otherwise, what kind of a story could I make up that would explain
all this?

Randy would know what I should do with my good fortune. And
it was good fortune, I thought with a big smile on my face.

Randy was at his shop as usual, located in a nearby strip mall. He
looked up as I walked in and said, "Hey, Matt."

With a big smile, I asked, "Are you in the mood to buy some coins
today?"

He laughed and asked, "You need some traveling money for a race
or something?"

"Something like that." Then I told Randy an abridged version of
how I found the coins and showed him the diary before opening
the bag.

From the look on his face, I could tell he was trying to figure out if

I had been drinking. But his look changed when I started pulling coins out of the bag.

I pulled out eight plastic bags with the ninety-four lower-value US $20 gold coins and laid them on the counter as Randy's eyes opened wide. With the coins in their separate bags, Randy could see them clearly. The look on his face showed me he understood the value of what he was seeing. When I pulled out the foreign coins I had not been able to identify and placed them on the counter, he gave a low, quiet whistle and stepped back. Randy had not yet touched a coin. When I pulled out the Spanish doubloons and slid them right in front of Randy's hand, he finally moved.

He slowly reached out, picked up a bag, and removed the first coin. He looked at it, then turned it over and looked some more. With his left hand, Randy picked up a magnifying loop and studied the coin. He put that one down, and did the same with half a dozen other doubloons, then the $20 coins. While he was looking at the coins on the table, I pulled out the rare $20 coins, hiding them in my hand. I had held these coins back, waiting until Randy had seen the rest.

When Randy started to weigh the coins, he still had not said a word. He looked at me with what I can only describe as being stunned. I opened my fist and showed him the rare coins. "Maybe you should check these out before you say anything,"

Randy took a quick look, then came from behind the counter, walked to the door and locked it, turning off the "open" sign as he did. "The shop is closed for the rest of the day. It's safer this way. I don't want anyone coming in interrupting us."

Randy walked back behind the counter and looked me straight in the eyes. "So, Matt, you really found these and the diary up in the mountains?"

"I did. I just got back from there."

He shook his head.

Excited, I kept talking. "Randy, I'm no coin expert like you, but before I came over, I looked online to get an idea of what these things might be worth. That is if they are real. These six were the ones that sent my head reeling. See what you think."

I handed Randy the six coins, and he carefully took them. He laid them on a cloth and examined them one by one. When he had looked at each one, Randy went to a huge book. He must have spent another thirty minutes looking at these last six coins and consulting the book. Occasionally Randy would make another low whistle or a sigh, but he did not say a word otherwise. I took his reaction as a confirmation that the coins were indeed real.

Randy placed the coins into rows. He took the ninety-four US $20 gold coins and arranged them into rows by date, the same as he had done with the other coins, except for three. The six rare $20 coins and five other coins Randy placed aside in their own grouping.

Then he finally spoke. "Matt, if you are looking to sell these, I can tell you I do not have enough money to buy them all." Then he laughed, a laugh filled with gravity and wonder.

I couldn't wait another second. "So, tell me, Randy, are these real?

"Oh, they are real."

"What do you mean?" I asked.

"What I mean is, these are the finest coins I have ever seen. These coins look like they have never been in circulation. Like the US $20 coins, they are all over 100 years old. Even the $20 coins that are not rare will bring soaring prices because they are so perfect. These coins look like they have been in a museum for the last 100 years. Wherever they have been, they are in perfect shape. The Spanish doubloons look like they are brand new. Every one of these coins will bring the highest prices."

Then he gestured to the ones he had laid aside. "You were right, the $20 coins are rare. But these other ones might even be rarer. I will have to do more checking, but I can predict these twenty coins are worth twice what the other 180 are."

"You are kidding me."

"Matt, if I were, it would be solid gold." He shook his head. "I think each of the coins you brought in will sell for twice what a coin of the same year would normally sell for because of their condition. Nine of the fourteen foreign coins I have set aside are from your

Spanish doubloons. These are so rare they are not in the book. The only reference is from a shipping manifest. All but three disappeared when the ship they were being transported on was reported lost at sea off the California coast in the 1700s. I cannot begin to imagine what they are worth, but I estimate it'll be in the millions.

"If this story is true and this Doug is promising you thousands more coins to find him, then we are talking billions of dollars worth of coins. The last five foreign coins are from France and are from a set. The set was supposed to be for President Lincoln as a gift for saving the Union. The wagon they were traveling on disappeared en route, and they disappeared. The six $20 coins are so perfect that any collector would pay two or three times the appraised value to own them without the Lincoln connection. Again, we are talking millions.

"Matt, you've got to get these coins somewhere safe and out of sight. If word of these coins hits the market, you could be in danger."

Now I was getting scared. "What? Why?"

"Because the kind of person who has the money to buy coins like these is not worried about the law, they just want the coins, and they might do anything to get them once they know they exist."

There went my dreams of having some ready cash for a search. "Well, what about selling the lower-valued ones so I have a bit of capital? That would give me a cushion while we look for a way to sell them without me being a target."

"OK, Matt, I do have a buyer that would love the $20 coins. I can then research an anonymous way into the higher-end market. I do have some connections with people who deal in that kind of coin. I can tell them a person brought them in after the death of a relative. This could take months to find safe buyers for the higher-end coins. These buyers operate outside the law, which means there will be no taxes and no press."

My mind was boggled at a coin market operating outside the law. But I'd ask about that later.

Randy's eyes narrowed, and he lowered his voice as if he was afraid of being overheard. "Matt, I am going to give you a partial payment of $50,000 right now for the $20 coins. That should hold you for a while. And I would suggest you go to the bank right now and put every coin I do not buy in a safe-deposit box. To tell you the truth, Matt, I would not want them in my safe for fear someone would come looking. We need to keep this on the down low, or we could both be in real trouble. That means we will have to sell each coin one by one. I will need to spread the coins around to all my dealer friends so no one is the wiser. I will tell them all that there are more coins coming, and if they want to be part of the deals, they need to keep quiet. That should hold them. Each coin dealer prides themselves on having great coins, and these qualify as great coins. How does that sound?"

"Sounds good. I'll take care of that today."

Then Randy leaned toward me and said, with a twinkle in his eye, "I'll make you a deal, Matt."

"What's the deal?"

"If you only go through me, I will do everything possible to keep your name out of the press. That will keep the feds out of your bank account and the press out of your backyard."

"But, what's in it for you, Randy?"

"What is in it for me is I will be the most famous coin dealer in the world. I do want the first pick of everything you bring in if you go rescue that guy. And, even if there are not any more coins in the future, you will be rich. I will make enough brokering the coins that I will be set for life myself." He folded his arms and, with a satisfied look, said, "I will write a coin book listing all the new coins I am selling. I can see a whole lot of dreams coming true for the both of us."

"I never even dared to have a dream like this, Randy. You really made my day."

"Made your day—this is making my life! It would be amazing if there is something real about the story and there are more coins."

"So . . ., are you serious about being able to get me the $50,000 today? I mean, if you don't have it, I can come back another day."

"Yes, I am serious." He looked through the ninety-four lower-end $20 coins and picked out twenty. He said, "OK, Matt, I have taken twenty of the $20 gold coins. I believe they will be worth at least $100,000 and maybe up to $200,000. I will take a lower cut than normal because the dollar amount is so high. I normally get 10 percent, but since you've agreed to go through me, I will only take 5 percent because this is such an incredibly large amount. Is that percentage OK with you?"

"OK is such a small word for so many dollars. I'll just say hell, yes!"

"It's a deal. When I have sold the coins, I'll give you the rest of the money for these twenty coins. By the way, can you come in on Thursday nights around 4:45? I close at 5:00. How about we plan to go to dinner once a week, regularly, like we are old friends and have been doing it forever. I'll tell you every week which, if any, coins to bring the following week. How does that sound?"

"That sounds much better than OK, but who's buying?" I said as we laughed and shook hands.

"Hold on a second." Randy disappeared into the back room.

When he came back out, he was carrying a big envelope and handed it to me, saying, "This should buy a pair of running shoes." He also handed me a receipt and said, "Now remember, Matt, don't put all this money into your bank account. You can only put a little at a time into your account, or you will owe the IRS. I would suggest putting the cash into the safe-deposit box too. Put only five or six thousand a month into your account. Don't go blowing it on cars, either. Keep a low profile for now. When the big money comes in, you will need financial advice, but for now, keep your head low."

"Will do. I don't need much anyway except maybe that new pair of running shoes."

"That's the attitude," he said as I went out the door, promising to return Thursday evening at 4:45.

When I got to my car, I got in and just sat there. Everything seemed unreal, even with the money in my pocket. Randy was right. I needed to keep all this quiet.

I drove to the bank and got myself a safe-deposit box. I kept $15,000 and put the rest in the box, plus all the coins. *I'm eating out tonight*, I thought, *and it's not going to be fast food.*

When I got done that night with a really nice dinner at an Italian restaurant, I was exhausted and headed my van home. It had been a long day and sleepless night before in my tree hammock in the mountains. Just before sleep, I thought about contacting Doug's mother. *I'll face that one tomorrow.*

3

I slept in, and over coffee the next morning, I thought about contacting Doug's mother. His note on the loose diary pages left her address and phone number. He hadn't asked the one finding the note to go see her in person. Maybe I'd just call her from a pay phone. No sense in letting her have my cell number. When I finished that, I would check out the maps Doug drew. I had all the maps of that area of the mountains at home, so that was no problem, and online maps would fill in blanks the maps didn't show.

While I drove to a nearby gas station to use a pay phone, I wondered what I should say. Should I mention the coins? The diary said the coins were mine for helping, but maybe his mother needed the money and would sue me for them. At the gas station, I dialed the number from the diary and got a "this-number-is-no-longer-in-service" recording.

I was going to have to go to her house and tell her in person. Crap! Now that I had to keep a low profile because of the coins, I really had to come up with a plan for what to say. There was no way I wanted to keep information from this woman about her son.

My own mother had died five years earlier from cancer, and I still missed her. I couldn't imagine what it would be like to have a son disappear in the woods and never know for sure what happened to him for six years. No, I had to go to the house and tell her. I got back into the car and headed to the address in North Seattle, only a couple of miles from my house.

But when I pulled up in front of the house and checked the number, I realized something was wrong. The house looked abandoned. The lawn hadn't been mowed, and the house looked like no one had been taking care of it. When no one answered the doorbell, I looked in the window next to the door. I could see some furniture inside, but I couldn't tell if anyone was living there. As I turned to go down the steps to the walk, I saw an older man standing on the sidewalk looking at me. He asked, "Can I help you?"

"Yes," I said, "I am trying to find Susan Wilson."

"Why?" he asked.

"Well, I have some news about her lost son."

"Oh," he looked down and got quiet. Then he said, "I'm her neighbor," by way of introduction. After a moment, he added, "I have some bad news. She died two years ago."

"God, I am sorry."

"Yes, it's sad. She waited and waited for him to return. She said she knew he wasn't dead. She just knew it. She got sick, and finally, she could not hold on. If you ask me, she died of a broken heart."

"Terrible," I muttered, not knowing what to say.

"Yes. She was so sure he'd be back she put the home in trust so it would be here for him when he came back. I never really thought he'd return, but the power of love a mother has for a son is strong."

I just nodded and kept silent.

"So, what do you know about her son?"

"Oh, a friend had heard he had been seen in Mexico. That's all I know." I felt bad about my lie, but it was the first thing that came to mind.

"Well, that is good news. I'll keep an eye out for him."

"OK," I said an awkward goodbye and walked to my car. As I drove away, I thought about Doug's mother, who died never knowing if her son was alive or not. I was feeling low but also relieved I did not have to tell her about her son. I told myself I shouldn't be feeling too bad because her son did say whoever found the backpack could keep the coins. And I was going to try and find him, after all.

Then I thought about the Sasquatch. I couldn't get my mind around real Sasquatch walking around. Were they real, or was it just a made-up story? Well, the coins were real. That much I knew.

My next step was to find out if there really were Sasquatch living in the woods. As I drove home, I thought about the hair Doug had put in the diary. The note said they were from five different Sasquatch. Even the hair from one real Sasquatch would be news, but five individuals? How could I find out what those hairs were?

Then I thought about my old friend Salli, a chemist who knows all about lab stuff. She could tell me where I could get the hair DNA evaluated. At home again, I waited until after 6:00, when I knew Salli would be off work, to give her a call. After a few minutes of catching up, I asked her where I could get animal hair DNA evaluated to see what species they were from.

"Matt, you trying to find out what breed your dog is? Or are you trying to see if you are human?" Salli laughed her head off at her cleverness, and I had to chuckle myself.

"No, I'm serious. I've got some animal hair I need tested."

"Okaaay . . . well, I think the lab my friend Bill Standish manages in downtown Seattle could do it," she said. "They evaluate genetic samples to see where various herds of deer and other mammals migrate and which ones are the top breeders. I'll give you his number at work and you can try him."

There was a pause, and Salli said, "So Matt, you going to tell me what you want evaluated, or do I have to beat it out of you?"

"Hey, girl! Why are you always so bossy?

"Only when I want my way."

"OK, OK, I will tell you. My friend saw a weird-looking troop of monkeys on an island in a swamp in Florida and wanted to know what they were."

"Cool," she said. "Well, that lab is the one to help you then. I know they have done stuff like that before. Just tell Bill I gave you his number and told you to call. Also, tell him he owes me a call. I have not talked to him in a while, and if you do business with him, he owes me."

"I'll give him the message. Thanks, Salli, it's been great talking to you."

The next morning I called Salli's friend Bill Standish and told him I had samples I wanted checked. He suggested I come by that afternoon, and I said I'd be there at 1:00.

I was excited about the prospect of finding out if the hairs were for real. My leg was feeling better, and I had four hours before the meeting, and the day was clear and warm, so I went for a run down at Seattle's waterfront. I liked running the waterfront because of all the parks and all the runners along the way that keep it interesting. My favorites were either there or around the almost three-mile circuit around Green Lake, which has a beauty all its own.

I arrived right at 1:00. As I walked into the building, I heard a voice call out my name. "Matt, Matt Hurley, I can't believe it is you!" I looked toward the man calling my name and did not recognize him. My lack of recognition must have been obvious by my face because he quickly introduced himself.

"I'm Bob Rogers. I recognized you, I've seen your races! I have been a runner for years, but not to Bill's level or yours."

I shook Bob's extended hand, "Nice to meet you. I thought we had gone to school together or something like that, and I had forgotten."

"Pleasure meeting you. I don't want to bother you, but I would love to talk running sometime."

We were still chatting when Bill Standish walked into reception from the back. Bob said, "Look who's here. I can't believe I get to meet Matt Hurley." Gesturing to Bill, he said, "Bill Standish—he's an elite runner too."

Bill and I shook hands, and I relayed Salli's message. The guy was all business. "So, what do you have for me? You didn't offer anything over the phone. But in this business, unless the customer offers, we do not ask."

I pulled out the hair wrapped in plastic from my pocket and handed it to Bill.

"A friend would like to have the species identified."

"Well, that is what we do here. Can you tell me a bit about where you got them?" Bill looked eager to get on with the identification.

"Sure. My friend found a small troop of strange-looking monkeys in Florida. He sent these hair samples to me and asked if I could have them evaluated to determine what species they are or if they are a new one altogether."

"It would be a cool find if it turns out they are from a new species," said Bill frowning. "Your friend would make the big time. Do you have any more information?"

"I would rather keep the information sparse until I find out if they are a new species."

"OK, Matt," said Bill, "sounds fair to me. The science community sometimes must keep things close to the vest to get the scoop. I would do the same in your position."

"I should tell you those samples are from five different monkeys."

"Thanks, Matt. I was looking at the hair colors in your sample, trying to figure out what we had here, and that helps. I will have my guys get on it as soon as they can. We should have the results in a couple of days."

I looked at Bill and said, "Is there any way, say, with more money upfront, you could rush the test?"

Bill looked at me, smiled and said, "Money always talks when you own a small business. We usually charge $5,000 to run those samples, but for $10,000, I can get you the results by 5:00 p.m."

That sounded fair, and I pulled out an envelope from my pocket and began counting out the hundreds as Bill openly stared.

"Um, Matt. Hold on a minute. Put that away for now. Let me make you a deal."

"What kind of deal?"

"Let's go to lunch and talk running. I will have my guys put the samples on five different machines, and we can run the tests in an hour. When we get back, you will have your answer, and I will have a chance to talk to one of my heroes about my favorite sport."

I was a little embarrassed, not being used to the attention. Elite runners didn't usually merit much press in the States. "OK, Bill, you have a deal. I just finished a twenty-miler and could use a bit more fuel. Also, it's always nice to talk to another runner."

Bill and I walked down the block and went into a local tavern Bill swore had the best hamburgers in Seattle, and he wasn't kidding. My double bacon burger with three different cheeses, three times the bacon, blue cheese, and a fried egg really hit the spot. We talked about running while eating, and Bill knew his subject. He and his lab crew were a bunch of fitness nuts who ran road races and raced bicycles. The lunch hour went quickly, and we were heading back to the lab in what seemed like minutes.

True to his word, the samples were ready when we got back. One of Bill's people was holding paperwork and talking excitedly to two other workers in lab coats. When he saw us enter the door, he almost sprinted to Bill.

Bill looked surprised and told the guy, "Slow down and talk English."

Without another word, the guy in the lab coat handed Bill a stack of papers. Bill glanced at the top paper, and me and his eyes opened wide. He skimmed through the stack, looked at the man in the lab coat and asked, "Did you rerun these tests?"

"Not only have we retested, but we have run three retests on different machines, and the results are always the same."

Bill thanked the tech and just stood there shaking his head. Finally, he turned to me and said, "We need to go into the back lab. You guys come with us," he gestured to the workers who gathered around.

Once we were all in the back lab, Bill looked at all his workers and asked, "Has anyone talked to anyone outside this building?"

There was a chorus of "No." The guy who had handed Bill the papers said, "We just finished the last retest when you came in the door. None of us has had a chance to do anything else."

"Thank God." Bill looked at his workers and said, "OK, guys, this is the biggest thing to ever happen to this lab. A once-in-a-lifetime happening. We can't let anyone know about this find. I am going to try to strike a deal with Matt here for exclusive lab testing rights to this find. That means this lab will be on the scientific map. I am letting you all know right now it means everyone in this lab will have an equal share in the findings and the press. You will all become known in our field, meaning all your dreams will come true. No more back-room lab work without recognition. It also means I promise to share the financial gains equally."

The looks on people's faces in the room ranged from disbelief to elation and everywhere in between. Bill went on. "But if this gets out early, we all lose. If we can keep our mouths shut, we all gain. Can I have your word that nothing goes outside this room?" He looked piercingly into the eyes of each one.

Now there were growing smiles on faces and heads began to nod, and the guys started saying, "Yes." Bill was offering an equal share in any profits and notoriety from this discovery, more than expected from such a find. It was like being on a relay team and breaking the world record. In the scientific world, notoriety and esteem were worth more than money, it was everything.

I stood by thinking, *These hairs have to be real. But what about that deal Bill said he was going to strike with me?*

Bill seemed satisfied with the response he was getting and turned to me.

"OK, Matt, now you need to tell me more. I am going to tell you the findings, but you must promise to tell me where you found them. I am also asking for the sole rights to DNA testing of any more samples. I would like to be able to publish all findings in the name of our lab. We will not publish or disclose any information until you say we can. Never mind about the $10,000 you were going to give me. And all future testing will be free. As far as we are all concerned, you are now a partner with this lab. This find means the world to our small lab. When the data is compiled, it will put this lab at the top of our field. All we are asking is that you fill us in on all the information you have, allow us to help in any way we can, and let us be the only lab that gets to evaluate all the future samples."

I looked at Bill and then looked at the eager faces around me and sighed. "All right, you have a deal," and we shook hands.

"Matt, I am guessing you know more than you told me about the samples."

"Yes."

"Before you say any more, I must say you were wrong. There are not five different samples, there are six. First, there are black hairs from a human male mixed in with the samples, which makes the sixth sample."

"That must be Doug, from the description in the diary," I said.

"Doug? Diary . . .? OK, now we have one of the samples identified. But none of the five other samples match any genetic sample known to man, and we have access to the complete bank of samples collected to date. That means these samples are from a completely new species and will knock the pants off the scientific community. Do you want to know why? Or, wait a minute, Matt . . . do you already know?"

"You tell me, Bill," I said.

Bill smiled and said, "Anyone want a beer?" The guys all said yes, and I followed suit. One of the guys ran to the refrigerator and brought out the beer left over from a party they had the week before. Bill commented, "I guess none of us is driving anywhere for a while if I read Matt's face correctly."

Bill smiled, opened his beer, took a big drink, looked around the room, and shook his head. "Matt," he said, "what we have is a mixed bag of results. It took a while to divide the samples up into the proper six specimen groups. There were three samples that were from the same species, and it is an unknown new species of humanoids. These humanoids are closely related to apes and man, but we split from them millions of years ago."

I nodded a bit and gave a little smile. I think he knew I had an idea where he was going with this.

Every eye in the room was on Bill as he continued. "From what we can tell, they are a distant relative of humans. I would guess somewhere around three million years ago, we split off from them, and that was after we had split off from the apes. That makes them closer relatives than chimpanzees. Chimpanzees are, or were, humans' closest relatives until these samples came into being. They are a 98.5 percent genetic match to humans. These samples are 99.2 percent match to humans. That is really close in genetic terms. Have you seen these subjects, Matt?"

"No, Bill, I have not, and I will get to that once you have finished telling me about all the samples."

"OK, that's fair."

"So now we know about the first three non-human samples. Non-human sample four is even stranger. It is even a closer genetic match to humans than the first three."

Surprised, I asked, "What do you mean by that?"

"Matt, the closest guess we can make from our tests is that somewhere between fifty and a hundred generations ago, or even one thousand to two thousand years ago, that sample subject's ancestor mated with a human. That means this sample is from a hybrid of a human and whatever this ape-like creature is."

All I could do was nod my head because it made sense from what I had read in the diary.

Bill looked at me for a long moment and said, "You don't look all that surprised, Matt. I will move on to the last and fifth non-human sample. Four non-human samples are from beings that may look more like humans than apes, but they will also still have a resemblance to apes as well. The fifth sample is different in two ways from the first four. First, it is a female. Second like the fourth sample, this creature is also a hybrid. The difference between her and the fourth sample subject is that she is a first-generation hybrid. This female is even more human than the first hybrid. Her father was a hybrid, but her mother was a full human. This hybrid female is approximately 99.75 percent human. I cannot even begin to guess what she looks like, except the samples indicate she is hairy, but I would expect her to look completely human. She will not be as hairy as a gorilla but thinner like a chimpanzee."

I was mulling this information over when Bill turned to me and said, "OK, Matt, I have told you everything we have learned. Now the ball's in your court. What can you tell us about the samples? Remember, you are in a safe place. We won't let this story out until you are ready."

I looked around the room at the guys holding their beer and leaning forward with intense expressions on their faces. "OK, it looks like you all are going to get the rest of the day off from work. The story I'm going tell you will take hours."

Bill looked at one of the guys and said, "Please shut the lab down and close the front door. We are going to have story time, and I don't want anyone coming in."

I waited until the man came back from locking up and for everyone to get comfortable and began.

"First, I found a diary while camping in the Cascades. There were some loose pages at the front of the diary. Those pages give the name of someone who was kidnapped and held prisoner—Doug. There was a map showing trails and caves. He had placed 200 gold coins into the backpack I found. The gold would go to whoever found the diary, so they would look for and rescue him.

"The map and loose diary pages are in my safe deposit box. I have already taken the coins to a coin dealer I know. They are in near-perfect condition and will bring higher prices than the coin world has seen to date. Some of the coins are extremely rare. My coin dealer friend estimates that the coins will bring anywhere from two to three million dollars."

I looked around the room and could tell I had everyone's interest. What is it about money that perks up interest?

"Yes, I said millions. Bill, that is where I got all that cash I tried to pay you with. The coin dealer fronted me $50,000 to hold me over until he could find buyers for the expensive coins. He has offered to sell the gold for me and only charged 5 percent instead of his normal 10 percent because of the worth of the coins. He is going to keep my finds secret because of the quality of the coins and what they can do for him as well. I haven't yet told him the whole story, the one that I am about to tell you."

"Doug's note said the 200 gold coins I found in the bag were just a down payment. If he gets rescued, he promises thousands more coins. I want to make you all a deal. Bill showed me he is a fair man by making you all equal partners in this discovery. I want to make you the same type of deal. I want to try to rescue this Doug and will pitch in cash to help pay for an expedition.

"I also want to make you all my partners in any of the gold we find. I will keep what I have already found. We can split any other treasures we may find equally between all members of this rescue and scientific mission. Each person in our group will get an equal share. I would also like to add my friend, the coin dealer, as an equal share partner because he will be the one helping us liquidate our coins. If we find Doug, we will all be richer than we have ever dreamed."

"Dang," said one of the guys, a short red-headed guy. "Can you imagine what kind of lab a person can build with that kind of money?"

"Yeah," said a tall guy with thick glasses. "Yeah, and I'd build my lab in the Bahamas!" The room erupted in laughter and speculation of what they would do with their money.

Bill broke up the chatter, "Ok, guys, let's listen to Matt's story before we spend money we don't yet have."

The guys settled down as I pulled the diary out of my bag, took a big swallow of my beer and began to read.

4

March, Day 1

Whoever finds this notebook, I am sorry if I'm rambling. I am not sure where to start. I was lucky they let me keep this notebook I found in one of their hoard caves. I call them hoard caves because they have been hoarding stuff for years. From the looks of the things in the caves, they have been collecting for thousands of years. More about that later. I want to tell you how I got into this situation.

My name is Doug Wilson. I was hiking in the Cascades, ten miles north of Snoqualmie Pass in Washington State, when I got injured. It was rough country, and I probably shouldn't have been hiking alone, but I wanted to take advantage of the light snowpack to get into the backcountry before the flies and humans got there. I was crossing a river on an old moss-covered log when I fell in. The river was running high and fast after three days of hard rain, which is normal in the Cascades in March. I was getting desperate because I had been trying to find a way across the river for hours. I know I should have been more careful, but then hindsight is always 20/20. Halfway across the log, a rotten piece covered by moss gave way, causing me to slip and fall into the freezing water.

I couldn't get my pack off. With my heavy pants, jacket, and boots, I didn't have much of a chance of staying afloat anyway. The current rolled me underwater and along the bottom. I was afraid I'd hit a rock and drown. It felt like forever as I was tumbling over rocks and going under again. Cartwheeling down the river, I heard a loud noise and caught a glimpse of a waterfall just ahead. I knew I was about to go over it and thought I was going to die for sure. While looking for a safe spot to cross the river, I got a better look at the falls. They were about forty feet tall, with huge rocks at the bottom. If the fall to the rocks below didn't kill me, the injuries from the fall would keep me from being able to swim and I would drown. As I approached the edge of the waterfall, the sound was almost deafening. I hit a large rock at the top, tumbled over it, and began falling.

My fall came to an abrupt stop. I heard a loud snap and felt a searing pain in my left shoulder. Somehow I had stopped and was hanging in midair on a branch that had become tangled in my backpack. The water was still rushing over me, but I was not falling. My right arm was not hurt and I was able to pull the hood of my rain jacket up over my head. That gave me a break from the water rushing over my face so I could breathe again. I couldn't see much because of the water going over the hood. When I looked down, I could see the sudden stop had left me hanging about ten feet from the bottom and the deadly rocks. No matter which way I tried moving my legs, they couldn't reach anything to stand on. I was hanging midair in the middle of a raging waterfall twenty miles from the nearest human.

I knew this was the end for me, and death would come quickly as the water was freezing cold. If I could not free myself, I would die within hours, if not minutes. My left shoulder felt dislocated, and my left arm felt broken. Without the use of my left arm, it was impossible to reach my knife to cut the waist belt or shoulder straps off the pack. The pack's waist buckle was too tight to undo with my full weight on it, and I couldn't lift myself and unbuckle it with just the use of one arm. Even if I could unbuckle it, the ten-foot fall onto rocks would be deadly. I was desperate to live, but I could see no way out of this situation.

After what must have been twenty minutes of hanging there, I was shivering and starting to become hypothermic. I knew once the shivering stopped, I would fall asleep, feel no pain, then die. I could feel myself getting sleepy and knew what was coming.

Then I woke up. It was dark, and I could not see or hear anything but the noise of the waterfall. I was still alive! Though soaked, My raingear and clothes must have kept me warm enough not to die. My silk long underwear, wool pants, and wool shirt under my raingear must have insulated me well. Maybe it's my size. At six foot, nine inches tall and 275 pounds, maybe it was taking longer to become hypothermic.

The pain in my arm and shoulder was not too bad because of the cold, but I still could not move the arm an inch. My left arm was useless. I was going to die, and no one would ever find me. I was way too deep into the wilderness anyway and far from human trails for anyone to ever chance upon me or my body. Someday, maybe, someone would find my remains hanging here.

The next time I awoke, it was daylight. It did not feel like I was awake, more like a dream. Two or three more times, I awoke and fell back asleep. I only remember the sound of the water and feeling cold. After that, I did not dream much, but I had the odd sensation of being lifted and moving, yet I had no control over it. I must have been in that freezing water for over twenty hours, and my mind was gone. I had dreams of soft fur and warmth. While I was in and out of consciousness, I felt like someone was hugging me. *Maybe this is heaven*, I thought. I am not sure how long I was out—or was I sleeping?—but it felt like days before my mind started to clear.

When I was finally able to open my eyes and could see clearly, I was unsure if I was awake, dreaming, or having a nightmare.

I was in a large cave, about ten feet from the opening, and it was light outside. My arm and shoulder were hurting, but surprisingly not badly. I was naked, and my arm was in a sling. I was lying in a soft bed, more like a nest of ferns and grass. I smelled something sweet; I was not sure what it was, but it smelled familiar.

By the length of the stubble on my face, I had been out for days, but I did not feel hungry. How had I gotten bandaged? And fed? I felt my forehead, but no, I didn't feel hot. No fever.

I looked around me at the cave, but it didn't look natural. The walls and floor were too smooth. And they almost seemed to be glowing. (I later learned that they spread a type of lichen that gives off a soft light. It was hard to notice in the daylight, but it made it easy to see and get around in the cave at night.)

I struggled to sit up but was still too weak to fully sit. But I propped myself up on my good elbow and looked around. In the faint light, I could see at least one hundred feet before the cave curved out of sight. There were at least five bed nests around me. I saw no sign of a fire, nor could I smell one. Whoever was in here didn't want anyone to locate them by smoke.

I lay back down and felt for my watch on my left wrist. The arm was indeed in a sling made out of smooth bark filled with soft grasses. Whoever did it had done an excellent job of immobilizing my arm. I moved the material from my wrist, and sure enough, I still had my watch. I pressed the light to check the time and could not believe what I saw. The time was 11:25 a.m., but the date must be wrong. If the date was correct, I had been unconscious and sick for over three weeks.

I lay back and thought about what must have happened. I was in a cave with grass and bark bandages, lying in a nest bed. *Must be a bunch of hippies that saved me.* As I began trying to make sense of what was going on, I felt tired again. I was not feeling as good as I thought because I fell back into unconsciousness again. The next time I woke, it was dark, and the cave was silent except for the sound of heavy breathing around me. I became aware that someone was sleeping up against me. There again was that sweet familiar smell. If it was the scent of a person, it smelled nice. I leaned toward them to take in the scent deeper. The smell seemed to come from a fur coat or blanket covering them. Once again, I fell asleep and snuggled up against that sweet-smelling person.

The next time I opened my eyes, it was daylight. The person in my bed nest was gone, but I could tell someone was still in the cave. I turned to see who it was and nearly stopped breathing. Ten or fifteen feet to my right was what looked like a bear squatting by the opening. My heart started pounding fast. What should I do? I felt too weak to get up, let alone get away from a hungry bear.

The bear must have heard me trying to move because it slowly stood up and turned around. I tensed and tried to scoot backward to get away from it. But I was not prepared for what I saw next.

It was not a hungry bear. I was unsure of what it was, but it scared the hell out of me so much I must have passed out. When I came to, it was still light, but there was not anyone or anything in the cave. I was alone.

I knew I had to try to sit up and get out of there before that thing came back. Whatever it was, it was big, and I was not taking a chance on it being friendly. I propped myself up on my right arm and tried to sit. It took effort, but after a couple tries, I was able to sit. The room was spinning, and my arm ached a little bit, but I tried to stand. I rolled over on my knees and tried to push myself up. I fell flat and felt pain in my arm, but I pushed myself up again. After a couple more tries, I made it to my knees. I was just feet from the wall, so I crawled over to it so it could aid me in getting to my feet. The smooth surface made it hard, but after a bit, I was standing. My legs were shaking, and I felt like I would fall at any time, but I stayed on my feet.

Once the spinning stopped, I made my way slowly to the cave opening. I did not see anyone outside, so I ducked under the overhang and went outside. I had not made it more than ten feet when I heard a sound. Someone was coming. I needed to get to the bushes quickly to hide. I only made it another few feet when something emerged from the trees just in front of me.

It looked something like a gorilla. I am tall at six foot nine, and this thing looked taller than me and heavier. And I could tell by the look on its face it was not happy.

5

The big hairy creature walked slowly towards me. It was like it could tell I was terrified, so it stopped ten feet in front of me and slowly crouched down. Then it started making soft mewing sounds. Its eyes softened as it looked at me. From the look on its face and in its eyes, I didn't think it would hurt me and even seemed concerned about me. It slowly reached out a hair-covered hand to me.

Then I found myself doing something crazy—I extended mine to it. With a calm and gentle touch, it held my hand. My fear subsided and I relaxed. It slowly stood without releasing its gentle grip on my hand while it looked at me with soft green eyes and smiled. I mean, it really smiled. It was like a human smile, but the face was hairy.

I looked closer at the creature holding my hand. Soft light-brownish-red hair covered its body and face. Those green eyes were as easy to read as human eyes, and I realized its face was almost human but with a bit more hair. Looking closer, I noticed it was a female. Being this close, I could smell her, the same sweet smell as the one that had been sleeping next to me.

She started making a soft mewing sound again and inched closer to me. She slowly brought her other hand to my hurt shoulder and touched it ever so gently. She tilted her head to the side and mewed again. The whole thing seemed like a dream, and I smiled. She smiled back and gently turned me back toward the cave.

I was in no position to argue and let her usher me back inside. Once inside, she moved me over to my bed nest. I took the hint and knelt. With gentle care, she helped me lie down and then covered me with dry long grasses, leaves, and ferns. She stood and walked to the side of the cave, picked something up and brought it over to me. It looked like a bowl and had something in it. She set the bowl down next to me, put her hand under my back and effortlessly lifted me to a sitting position. With her free hand, she scooped out a small amount and held it to my lips. I took the hint and ate. To my surprise, it was good. It tasted like nuts and sweet berries with a hint of potatoes. She seemed pleased, and I relaxed more.

I don't remember falling asleep, but when I awoke again, I felt much better. My arm and shoulder were not sore at all. I knew my arm had been badly broken, yet I almost felt completely healed. Whatever she had done, my broken arm had somehow healed months earlier than normal.

I sat up easily and looked around. I was in the same cave as before. No one or thing was around, so I got to my feet. I was naked and started looking around for my clothes. All I found were a few bowls and baskets. My clothes were nowhere to be found, so I gave up and went outside naked. It was still April, but the sun was shining, and I didn't feel too cold.

Outside I saw another huge furry creature over by a log. It glanced at me, then looked away. It looked different than the one that had slept by me and fed me. Its hair was longer, thicker, and looked more like fur than the female that had been taking care of me. This new hairy beast was also much bigger than the first female. I assumed this one must be a male because of the larger size and denser fur. Whatever it was, it paid no attention to me.

I felt a bit scared and tried not to move too fast, but I wanted to see where I was. Outside the cave was a small clearing. I guess it was about fifty feet across and clean as a park. There were logs in a circle but no fire pit. These animals must not have fire, but somehow I knew they were intelligent. My quickly healing arm and shoulder were a testament to that.

As I looked around, another of the large furry beings entered the clearing. It looked at me for a second, then walked into the cave carrying a basket made of grass or bark.

As I watched it and looked back at the one by the log, my eyes widened as I suddenly realized what they were. These had to be Sasquatch or what the local Native Americans called Sasquatch. That was the only thing they could be. Yes, they were Sasquatch, and I was in their camp.

Just then, the one who had been caring for me walked into the clearing carrying a basket. I swear she smiled when she saw me. She immediately came over to me and looked me over as if she were checking to see if I was OK. She tilted her head to the side, gently placed a hand on my bandaged shoulder, and again made a soft mewing sound. I could tell by her worried expression and the mewing she was asking how I was.

I looked into her eyes, nodded and smiled. That seemed to satisfy her, and she went into the cave. In less than a minute, she was back at my side. She made hand gestures like she was feeding herself and pointed at me.

Is she asking if I am hungry? I shook my head to indicate no and rubbed my belly.

She seemed to understand and again gave me a little smile. Then she gently held my good arm and tugged me towards the circle of logs. I gathered she wanted me to sit because she sat and pulled down on my arm. Once I was sitting, she began running her fingers through my hair, which was weird, but I sat still.

I had now seen only three Sasquatch. They were all covered with hair, but it was not long. My hair was long, down to my waist, and I had a full beard. I looked like them, especially because I was so tall and hairy. I had been teased my whole life for being hairy, but here I looked almost bald in comparison. I had forgotten I was naked until the female ran her fingers through my thick chest hair as if she was comparing my hairy body to hers.

My Sasquatch friend seemed fascinated with my long hair and kept running her fingers through it. My hair is black and very thick, and from what I had seen so far, an unusual color and length.

I thought of a study I had read of female lionesses in Africa using two stuffed fake male lions with manes. One had a light mane and the other a dark full mane. The lion with the dark mane was the one that attracted the lionesses the most.

I assumed she was fascinated with me because of my hair. I was also wondering what she thought of my light blue eyes. I felt like she was displaying nurturing behavior.

I didn't mention this, but I am a psychologist specializing in behavioral psychology. At least, I assumed that was what she was doing. Whatever she was doing, I didn't feel in any imminent danger.

But what she did next did surprise me. She got up and gently pulled me to my feet. Holding me by my arm, she led me out of the clearing into the woods. I didn't know where she was taking me, but I am sure I had no choice. I don't think I could have stopped her even if I were fully healthy.

We came to a small river about twenty-five or thirty feet across and about four feet deep. It was slow-moving and didn't make much noise, which is why I had not noticed it before. She stopped at the edge of the river and looked at me. Then she waved a hand in front of her face and covered her nose. It took a few seconds, but I realized what she was trying to say. I stank!

Considering how sweet she smelled, I could see why she thought I needed to bathe. The last time I would have washed myself was over three weeks before when I fell into the river. I took a whiff myself, and sure enough, I stank to high heaven.

I must have made a face when I smelled myself because she suddenly let out a laugh. There was no mistaking that it was a laugh. I knew apes laugh, so this didn't seem strange to me. Her laughter eased the tension I was feeling about my situation.

She looked me in the eye, tilted her head, and made a face that looked like it was curious.

Then she motioned to the river with a nod of her head and walked into the center of it herself. After almost dying in the last river, I wasn't really looking forward to going in, but I didn't think she'd have let me get away without a bath. From her slight frown, I could tell she was getting impatient.

The first step was the hardest because it was cold, but I knew I had no choice but to keep moving. I walked out to where she stood, and it wasn't that bad. Then she cupped her hand and slowly poured water over my bad shoulder. I was amazed at how gentle she was. It was like getting bathed by a nurse in a hospital, except this nurse was very large and hairy.

I thought my hands were big, but hers were huge. She could cup quite a bit of water and quickly had me wetted down. I had not seen her pick it up, but she had moss in one hand, and she began scrubbing me with it. Now I knew where the sweet smell came from that I smelled on her and the bed nest.

It was strange, but from what I had read of the Sasquatch always mentioned their bad odor. I don't know where that urban myth came from, but this one smelled great. As she washed me, I noticed the moss cleaned as well as soap. *What a weird commercial for a natural soap this scene would make,* I thought. I must have been smiling because she smiled back. It felt wonderful to feel clean again.

After my bath was complete, she helped me to the shore as she must have noticed I was beginning to tire. My hairy nurse gave me a look that communicated *stay* and walked over to a large moss-covered tree. She returned with two handfuls of moss and proceeded to dry me with the unbelievably soft, sweet-smelling moss.

I was starting to get shaky standing by then, and she first helped me over to a patch of grass in the sun to rest and then back to my bed nest. When I awoke, I was warm and comfortable and felt like I had been wrapped in a fur blanket. The soft fur felt good against my naked back, and as I tried to snuggle tighter into the blanket, it started to move. I was back in my nest bed and my lady Sasquatch was holding me. She was so big it was like being held by my mother when I was a small child. I felt warm and quite comfortable, and the warmth and comfort lulled me back to sleep.

* * *

I heard sounds as I started coming out of my dream. In the dream, I was still in the river under the waterfall, and a huge hairy monster was trying to get me. The sounds grew louder. I lay there, not moving, just listening.

It sounded like a bunch of odd syllables thrown together, like when a two-year-old is babbling. Without opening my eyes, I took inventory of myself. My arm and shoulder felt fully healed. I felt better than I had in years. Whatever they were feeding me obviously was healthy. I was still naked but did not feel cold. It was hard to feel shy being naked when everyone—or everything—around me was also naked. Too bad I didn't have more body hair. If I was here in the winter, the rain and snow were going to be hard on me without clothes.

I wondered, *would my Sasquatch nurse give me my clothes back if I asked?*

Opening my eyes to see who was doing the vocalizations, I saw three Sasquatch standing close together, talking near the entrance of the cave. I could see another two outside the cave sitting in the log circle, who appeared to be weaving intricate baskets out of grass.

I sat up to get a better look at the cave and what was going on around me. As I did, the three in the cave, who were larger and looked like males, stopped talking and looked at me. My nurse was not one of the ones talking.

One of them looked at me, turned to the others and said something, then walked out of the cave. The one that left the cave walked across the clearing and disappeared into the woods without turning around. He came back within ten minutes with a large basket and emptied it at my feet without a word.

The basket contained a wide selection of clothes, shoes, boots, backpacks, and other assorted gear. Half the stuff was old, like antique woodsmen gear, but some looked brand new. Sorting through, I found my own boots and my clothes, for which I was deeply grateful because I wear a size fourteen shoe, a larger size than most.

I quickly put my clothes and shoes on, happy I had enough to keep me warm, dry, and comfortable, no matter the weather. There were dozens of packs in the basket, and I found a lightweight one that would work well. I found two Leatherman-type tools, a flint starter, and a good med kit, not that I was worried, but I might need a bandage occasionally. I finished off my pack with a good rope at least two hundred feet long but slim and lightweight. The pack I picked had a built-in poncho, so I would be ready for rain.

If I would be with them that long.

After I was dressed and was tying up my pack, my lady Sasquatch came into the clearing. She smiled when she saw me dressed and ready to leave. Perhaps we would soon be moving on. By the way they were acting restless, and with the increased activity I had noticed around me, I had felt for days they were just waiting for me to heal before they moved on.

6

I t had been about six weeks since I had been with the Sasquatch, and my arm had been out of the sling for about two weeks. I am unsure how she did it, but my broken arm and dislocated shoulder healed twice as fast as they should have.

It was mid-April, and the weather was really starting to get nice. I noticed my friend was rapidly losing her coat of fur. Substantial portions of her body now were only lightly covered with hair. Her skin was light brown and smooth. She looked like a well-built, athletic human female but with the strength of a male professional basketball player. I kept thinking the WNBA would go nuts for this lady.

When she caught me looking at her body, she smiled, and I am sure I blushed. I could not believe I was looking at an ape and thinking she looked good.

I was jolted out of my trance when she motioned for me to follow her as she walked out of the clearing and into the woods. We appeared to be on a game trail, a well-kept game trail without potholes, washouts, and greenery or brush. This trail looked like someone had been keeping it clear. I guessed the Sasquatch had used this trail for a long, long time and had learned to keep the trail clear for easier traveling.

The trails we took always kept us below the ridge line, except in rare cases when we had to go over a ridge. If we had to go over a ridge, they always did it under the cover of trees and brush. This troop of Sasquatch really knew how to travel undetected. It was easy to see why almost no one ever saw them.

We stopped every few hours as they did not seem to be in much of a hurry. Maybe they were going easy on my account. But they were not grumbling at me for slowing them down and just seemed happy to be moving.

In the late afternoon, after two days of easy walking, foraging, and resting relaxedly, a new young male visitor Sasquatch hurried up to my lady Sasquatch and stirred things up a bit. They hugged and laughed, then started talking but in different vocalizations than I had heard before. The sounds were ape- or chimp-like, but they had a highly organized structural formation.

They spoke for a few minutes, then abruptly hugged and said their goodbyes. The young male looked at me for a few seconds, then quickly ran back in the direction he had come from.

The change in the troop's excitement was apparent. The pace quickened and they spoke among themselves more than they had the whole time I had been with them. In the beginning, I didn't know they used language because they didn't speak around me much until we left on the trip.

The next morning, we were up early and moving much quicker than before. I felt great and enjoyed being pushed for the first time since falling into the river six weeks earlier.

We had been walking for a few hours that morning when I saw something in the distance on our trail heading towards us—more Sasquatch were approaching.

As we got closer, I could tell it was another troop of Sasquatch, but it looked like they had smaller young ones with them. As they drew even closer, I could tell there were two humans with them! I was elated. *Surely I would be let go.* At least I would have someone to talk to for the first time in six weeks.

As we approached them, my friend put her hand out in front of me and I could tell she wanted me to stop. I had learned my lesson before when she just picked me up and put me back where she wanted me to stay. So I stayed while she walked forward to meet the new troop.

After they had talked together in their undiscernible communication, she motioned me forward. As I did, everyone in the new troop really gave me the once over. Two of them walked up to me and ran their hands through my hair. There it was again—my hair seemed to be the main center of attraction.

Then one of them waved to a short, young human, and he came forward. The Sasquatch that had called him over talked to the human for a bit as the human looked at me. My lady Sasquatch spoke to him in her language, and he spoke it back to her.

He must have been with them long enough to learn their language, I thought and wondered if that, too, would be my fate. He chuckled as my lady Sasquatch talked to him. With a final short exchange and a slight bow, he turned to me.

"Hi," he said, "how are you?"

"Fine . . . now . . ." I said although I was beginning to wonder if that was strictly true. "Who are you?"

"My name is Mike," he replied, "but my hairy friends here call me Crazy Goat."

"Goat . . . hello Mike . . . um Crazy Goat. I'm Doug. So, uh, Mike, can you fill me in a bit as to what is going on?"

"What is going on is you are on display. Daru is showing you off."

"Daru? Her name is Daru? Showing me off? But why?"

"Well, you are their biggest find in quite a while. It's your size . . . and the color of your hair."

"OK, but what does that mean?"

"Doug, this is going to sound weird, but they expect you to be Daru's mate. After all, she found you."

"What? No way, man! There is no way I am going to get that friendly with an animal."

"Take a look around. Do you think you have a chance of getting away? Hell, man, I have been with them over forty years and have never even gotten close to getting away, and I am no catch like you."

"What are you talking about? How could you have been with them for forty years? You hardly look thirty or thirty-five at most."

Mike said, "I was thirty-two when they found me hurt after a car accident. I was hurt badly, and they nursed me back to health. I hate to tell you, but once a human is taken in with them, they are not allowed to leave. The risk of being found out or of being hunted is too great." He gave a little laugh and continued, "But one of the side benefits is they live many times longer than us. And we live for a long time when we live with them.

"Now I am seventy-seven years old and in better shape than when I was in the accident over forty years ago. Sometimes I want out of here, Doug, but other times this life is perfect. You never get sick. You live well for a very long time. There is no stress about jobs or money, and everyone around is nice."

Shaking my head as if I could make the reality of all this go away, I asked, "Where did they find you?"

"I was with a group of friends backpacking in the backcountry when one of the guys had a run-in with a bear. He was hurt badly, and we were taking him out when we got into a car accident right by a river. I am not sure what happened to the others because I was thrown from the back of the truck where I was holding my injured friend Randy.

"My hairy friends found me a day after the accident, floating in the river two miles downstream. I don't know what happened to Scott, Randy, Jerry, and Rick."

"I am sorry," I said, but by then, I was starting to feel sorrier for myself.

I looked around at the peaceful Sasquatch mingling about and asked, "But why do they call you Crazy Goat?"

Mike looked at me and started to smile, but within seconds his smile had become a roaring laugh. His laughter soon attracted the attention of the Sasquatch, and they moved closer to where Mike and I were standing. He saw me look at them, slapped my shoulder, and said, "Don't pay any attention to them. They understand English and can talk it when they want to, but they want me to talk to them in their language, except for the rare times I'm with other humans. But they really enjoy hearing me tell the story of how I got my name.

"OK, let me set the stage," he said. "First, you got to understand these big guys are stronger than any ten men. A big guy like you would have a problem with even a young one. Good thing they are gentle and peaceful, or they would be dangerous. As you may have noticed, I am short. I stand five feet two inches tall. Around these seven-foot giants, my height was something of a joke when they first found me.

"After I had been with them six months and healed, I noticed one of the young males was saying derogatory things about me. By then, I had picked up some of their language, enough to understand conversations. The next time I heard him do it, I got a little angry. Finally, I had enough and I lost my temper. Call it short-man syndrome if you want, but I had enough.

"Anyway, as I said, these giants are peaceful. I have never seen one of them mad or lose their temper, so having this young male pick on me was out of character. I heard others tell him to be nicer to me. He'd just laugh, do something irritating, and talk trash about me, not knowing I could understand what he was saying.

"One day, we were gathering branches for the evening sleep when he started in again. He was calling me a 'tiny human child' and saying they should save the kid's branches for me. That might not sound like much, but I must have been overly tired or frustrated because I started yelling at him. I started yelling in English, then switched to Sasquatch. He was laughing until I switched to Sasquatch, then it got serious. In fact, all the Sasquatch in the area stopped talking and just watched and listened.

"We had stopped at a favorite place about sixty feet above a picturesque lake and had been gathering branches. They chose this spot deep in the Cascades because of the availability of water and the lack of humans. The trail we were on had a wide spot that was about thirty-five feet across, and the young male and I were on opposite ends.

I started yelling at him, calling him a "big pile of deer droppings" and other choice things, like 'You smell like a forest fire." Believe me, those are bad names in Sasquatch. He started to get upset, which is something I hadn't seen in a Sasquatch. Suddenly, he started running toward me. Thirty-five feet to travel is nothing when you are seven feet tall. I don't know what possessed me, but I started running at him as soon as he started toward me.

"I really don't think this group of beings had ever seen one of their own lose control, and they just looked on frozen. Just before we collided, I realized what was about to happen. I don't know what I was thinking, but I bent over and head-butted the running Sasquatch," Mike said with a big grin.

As he got to this part of the story, I could hear the Sasquatch around us making soft laughing sounds like snickering.

"Well, when a five-foot-two-inch man and a seven-foot man hit head-on, the five-foot man's head does not hit the seven-foot man in the head."

At this part, the Sasquatch started to laugh a bit louder and began rocking back and forth. Mike looked at me, watching the Sasquatch, and said, "Yes, they really like stories and have an enthusiastic sense of humor, especially if it is meant kindly."

He wasn't finished with his story. "So, if a five-foot-two-inch man runs bent over and hits a seven-foot-tall Sasquatch, it is right in the family jewels. And even a Sasquatch has a weakness or two. That young male must have weighed 290 pounds, and I weighed about 175, so that was over 450 pounds colliding at a vulnerable spot at about thirty miles per hour.

"The impact stopped him in his tracks, and he stood up as straight as an arrow. I stopped abruptly, too and fell backward on my butt. I looked up at the Sasquatch standing as still as a statue when suddenly his eyes rolled back, and all I saw was the whites of his eyes."

The murmurs and laughter from the crowd of Sasquatch around us kept building as Mike kept talking. "Next thing I know, the young Sasquatch started swaying back and forth. He was out cold but had not fallen. As he was swaying, I could see his eyes were beginning to flutter, and he appeared to be awakening. He looked down at me, said something, made an angry face, and stepped forward toward me. Well, his head was not fully clear, and he stumbled past me, staggering around the trail like a drunk man. To his great misfortune, we had ended our argument ten feet from the cliff edge over the lake, and he was stumbling straight toward it. No one was close enough to grab him and I watched with mixed emotions as he went over the edge and plunged sixty feet to the lake below.

"I figured the chilly water would wake him and was surprised at the reaction of the other Sasquatch. They were acting like going over the cliff would kill him. It was only sixty feet to the bottom, there were no rocks to land on, just deep, still water. He was built like a tank, so the landing shouldn't have hurt him a bit, just soak and embarrass him.

"The Sasquatch seemed frozen in their tracks, so I jumped to my feet. I was feeling fine as I had spent my whole life playing rough, including eight years of football. Being shorter than the other players meant I hit under the guard of the bigger players and inflicted greater damage than they could inflict on me.

"None of the Sasquatch were moving to save their comrade, so I figured it was up to me. I sprinted to the edge of the cliff and saw the Sasquatch thrashing in the water below, unable to keep his head above water. At that point, the physics of the situation became apparent. Sasquatches weigh too much to be able to swim well. That must be the reason they never go into water deeper than waist deep.

"I noticed one of the Sasquatch had dropped a rope it had been carrying when the fight first broke out, and I ran to pick it up. With rope in hand, I ran back to the cliff edge, kicked off my boots, dropped my pack, threw off my coat, and leaped off the cliff. As I went over the edge, I could hear the gasps of the Sasquatch as I plunged into the cold mountain lake below. My plan was to throw the rope around him and pull him to shore. The problem was the shore was almost fifty feet away and this guy weighed 300 pounds and was going to sink soon. I landed about twenty feet from the drowning Sasquatch and swam as close as possible without giving him a chance to grab me so he couldn't pull me under, trying to save himself. While treading water, I tied a loop on one end of the rope, then let the rest of the rope uncoil in the river current. My idea was to throw the loop over the Sasquatch's shoulders and tow it to shore. After a few tries, it became apparent I would never get the rope around him while he was struggling so frantically. Time was running out—the young Sasquatch was going to drown about ten feet away from me.

"His head went under for the last time. His thrashing arms went limp and then slowly slipped beneath the water's surface. I took a few deep breaths and dove beneath the lake's clear surface. When I reached him, I slipped the rope over its head, slid it under those long furry arms, pulled the loop's slip-knot tightly around the huge chest. and pushed off the bottom to head for the surface.

"I swam toward the shore, hauling the full weight of the unconscious Sasquatch, almost pulled under myself. Swallowing water, I was coughing and choking, but I was determined not to give up. I was responsible for the Sasquatch falling off the cliff, and I would have been dead if it were not for the Sasquatch saving my life.

"When I was about ten feet from the shore, a long hairy arm reached past and grabbed the rope. That long hairy arm was connected to one of the bigger Sasquatch I had ever seen, and he had stepped into the water deeper than waist deep to help. He grabbed the rope and began pulling hard on the rope until the limp body of its fellow Sasquatch was on shore. All the Sasquatch stood around him and wailed, beating their chests, one dropped to its knees next to the body wailing.

"Without thinking, I stepped up to the unconscious body and yelled at the kneeling Sasquatch to move. I knelt next to him, tilted his head back, checked for obstructions, and then began mouth-to-mouth resuscitation, alternately beating rhythmically on his chest. There was dead silence around me as I did. After a minute, the Sasquatch began moving slightly, then suddenly threw up a gallon of water. The Sasquatch was choking and sputtering, but he was breathing. He was going to live!

"The male leader of the troop stood over the soaked and subdued youngster and spoke to it in a quiet deep tone. Then the leader reached a long hairy arm down and offered me a hand up. He lifted me with ease and looked into my eyes, surprising me by speaking English. 'Crazy Goat is what you shall be called from now on. You have the heart of a goat. You took on a tormenter twice your size and won. You also showed us your honest heart by risking your life to save the life of my only son. I owe you a debt.'"

Mike said, "I was speechless and wondered what he meant."

The leader said, "I am offering you two choices. You can leave us and go back to your world, or you can stay with us. You will be afforded all the freedoms the rest of us have. Over time you will learn too much about our culture, so you will never be able to leave and go live with your people. You will be free to study and travel with us. Your life will be healthy and exceptionally long. But, if you choose to leave, I ask that you never reveal our existence. But whether you leave or stay, I beg you to show us that breathing thing you did to save him. It is something we have not known about, and it could help us in the future."

"Great story," I said. "How do you get along now with the young man you saved?"

"That's another story," Mike said. "He came to me after he recovered and asked me to forgive him for being cruel. And then he offered to be my helper for the next month—he called it the next moon—as penance for his unkind deeds. He said he'd teach me all I needed to know to easily live among the Sasquatch. And he offered to help me get better with the language.

"He told me, 'Goat, they call me Shrew because, among my kind, I am small and often in a bad mood. My goal is to develop the calm you showed while I was being unkind.'

"I took Shrew's huge hand in mine and said, 'Shrew, I accept your offer, but it will be as equals or not at all.'

"Shrew smiled and bent down, wrapped his long arms around me, and picked me up, holding me in a tight hug that made me quite uncomfortable. When he put me down, I looked at him and said, 'Friend, you will always be my equal.'"

The Sasquatch that had been listening to Goat's story nodded and laughed a bit more as Mike finished his story, then they drifted away.

Mike looked at me and said, "These Sasquatch are wonderful beings. You will learn much on your own and by talking to the other humans you will meet. There are quite a few humans living with the Sasquatch. A few have been living with them for well over a hundred years. This may not be your old life, Doug, but I promise it will be peaceful. You will learn many things that will make you rethink everything you know about humans. These Sasquatch have been on earth as long as we humans. The difference is they have not changed much physically in three million years, but they sure got smart. Don't be fooled, Doug, these guys are much smarter than humans."

"So what did you decide? Stay or go? You're still here, so I guess you chose to stay."

Mike looked at me steadily for a few moments, then said, "Doug, I really wanted to go home, and I am sure it would have been better for my family, but I loved being with the Sasquatch and the chance to learn was too much of a temptation to resist. So forty-two years ago, I decided to run away from my old life and stay here."

"Don't you miss your family and your old life?"

"Don't get me wrong, Doug, I still wish I knew what happened outside of my family and old life, but I don't regret my decision to stay. I wasn't married and didn't have any kids, so there was not much I was giving up. I expect the next couple of centuries will bring me the satisfaction of discovery and the time to forget the past."

I looked at Mike and asked, "Do you think there is any chance I would ever be let go?"

Mike's eyes looked kind but deeply sad and he said quietly, "No. I am sorry to tell you that no one I have ever talked to has ever known about anyone being released in the last one hundred years. The Sasquatch have a great fear of humans finding out about them and hurting them. The best advice I can give you, Doug, is to relax and be thankful that Daru found you and not someone else."

"Why is that?"

"Daru is mostly human and rare among the Sasquatch because she sheds her hair every year and looks human," said Mike. "Haven't you noticed Daru is shedding now?"

"Well, yeah. It's hard to miss."

Mike said, "Daru is one of the most beautiful females I have ever seen. Only when she is covered with hair does she look a little like an animal. You'll see what I mean in a few weeks, and you will change your tune. Oh, for sure, you will change your tune. Those big green eyes and that beautiful face will have you singing another song soon."

We sat and talked for the next few hours until a large Sasquatch walked up and spoke to Mike in Sasquatch. Mike answered him, and the Sasquatch left. Mike looked at me and said, "It's time you saw something of the way these Sasquatch really live. Come with me, Doug," and took off walking into the forest.

7

I followed Mike for about fifteen minutes before he stopped and said, "Here we are, kid. What I am about to show you is a small example of Sasquatch technology."

"Sasquatch technology? From what I had seen, I wouldn't exactly have put together those two words."

"Well, keep your eyes open. This is a storehouse that the Sasquatch use for what they find. From what I can guess, some of the things in here the Sasquatch have made. I can point identify most of the stuff they have found and stored, but I can't always identify the Sasquatch items they have made themselves. You will have a better idea than me since you have been outside in the last forty-two years. I haven't seen a newspaper or heard a radio in that time."

Without another word, Mike turned to his right, walked face-first into a large tree, and disappeared. *What the . . . ?* I walked over to the tree and looked at it closely. The tree looked real enough, so how did Mike walk right into it? I carefully reached out to touch the tree, and as my fingers got within a few inches from the tree, a phantom hand suddenly shot out of the tree bark and grabbed my hand. I screamed, and the sound seemed to be coming from somewhere inside the tree.

I jumped and desperately tried to pull away. The hand let go, and

I stumbled back and almost fell on my butt as I fought to regain my balance. Then I heard Mike's loud booming laugh and a few others laughing around him. *My new friends, the Sasquatch, were having a great laugh at my expense*, I thought, my face growing red.

Mike stuck his head out from the side of the tree with a huge grin on his face. "That's what happened to me when they first showed me the tree. It's like an initiation or something." He turned around, headed back toward the tree, looked at me, and said, "Come on," then disappeared back into the tree.

I cautiously walked back over to the tree. As I reached my hand out to touch the tree, my fingertips went right through the tree with just the faintest sensation of a breeze. The rest of my body went through as easily as my hand. Once my face came through the invisible wall, I could see I was in the entrance of a cave. It appeared to be like the cave I woke up in weeks ago, but this cave was much larger. Like the other one, this one had a light glowing from a kind of moss that retains light.

We were in a large chamber at least a few hundred feet long in either direction. The walls slowly curved until they went out of sight. I wondered if these caves were much longer than I could see. I turned around to look back at the tree that I had just come through and was surprised to see an open door that appeared to be made from rock.

Mike told me, "The door hidden behind the fake tree will open only if the person going through is supposed to go through. If you are not supposed to go through, it will not open, and the tree will feel as real and hard as a normal tree. I don't know how it works, but I believe it is a very advanced science that humans do not yet possess. I told you they were smart."

The wall opposite the doorway I had come through had many more rock doorways like that one. Set twenty to fifty feet apart, they continued along the wall as far as I could see. Some doorways were the width of a normal doorway, except they were taller to allow for the seven-foot-tall Sasquatch. Other doorways were wide enough to drive a pick-up truck through.

Mike told me, "Those are for the silent truck-like vehicles they use to move very heavy objects."

The sheer number and size of doors we passed made me wonder what was behind them. Mike stopped in front of a warehouse door, about twenty feet wide by twenty-five feet tall, with no apparent handle or lock. He placed his hand on the rock door, and instantly the door silently slid up into the ceiling. The light was a bit lower in this room due to the higher ceiling, so it took a few seconds for my eyes to take in what was behind the door. I was shocked to see a room full of tables covered with all kinds of goods. In the room that looked to be about forty feet wide and hundreds of feet deep were tables full of canned food, camping equipment, and electronic equipment from phones to TVs.

I told Mike, "This looks like a giant swap meet! Where did this stuff come from?"

"This is nothing. It's just one of thousands of rooms like it. It's a sorting room. When the Sasquatch find something, they bring it to one of these caves to be sorted, identified, and placed into the proper storage cave with other similar items. This is where having a human who has just come in from the outside helps. Those of us who have been out of circulation for a while do not know the function of many of the things coming in."

Mike looked at me and said, "This is where you'll come in handy. Well, that is until you have been here long enough not to know the latest technology."

I didn't know what to think of what Mike was saying. He was assuming I was going to stay and work with the Sasquatch.

Mike didn't seem to notice. He said, "I am hoping you can tell me what you think of the gadgets the Sasquatch make. I want to know what they are and how they work. I know many of them are electronic, but I have no idea what they are. I'm trying to figure out why the Sasquatch are making and storing them."

I must have had a puzzled look on my face because Mike said, "Yes, Doug, they can and do make things. The Sasquatch have made some high-tech stuff like the fake trees and weird things that I just cannot comprehend what they are or what they are used for."

As I looked around the room, he continued, "These sorting caves are just the beginning. If you think this is something, follow me."

I followed Mike out the door and down the hall. He stopped at a large door about nine feet tall and six feet wide. Doug watched Mike place his hand on the door, and it, too, retracted silently up into the ceiling. Inside the room, which was about twenty feet wide by eighty feet deep, were shelves about eight feet tall and four feet wide. Mike said, "Doug, go ahead and investigate some of those boxes on the shelf over there."

I walked up to the closest shelf and saw that the shelf held what appeared to be many stone boxes with stone lids. I glanced back to Mike, who nodded for me to open one. Reaching for a box on a shelf nearest me, I was surprised to find the stone was too heavy to pick up. Realizing it would be too hard to move the whole box, I thought I'd try removing the top. The top looked the same as the rock walls, boxes, and shelves, so I was prepared for the lid to be heavy.

But when I lifted it, the top was as light as a paperback book, and it pulled off so hard it flew out of my hands and skidded across the floor. It sounded like plastic or glass as it hit the floor and banged to a stop. Surprised, I tried to figure the whole thing out. I thought it was the box itself that was heavy and now discerned it must be the contents of the box. Would that mean that the boxes, tops, walls, and doors were all lightweight glass or ceramics the Sasquatch had made? I was beginning to believe Mike about the intelligence of the Sasquatch.

When I peered inside the box, what I saw made my knees go weak, even though the lighting was dim.

The box was full of gold coins. I couldn't help myself and reached into the box, pulling out a few of the heavy gold coins. I reached back in, pulled a few more coins out of the box, looked at them for a few seconds, and then put them back. Every coin in the box was a $20 gold piece from 1899. I looked around for the top of the box I had accidentally flung and put it back on the box. My curiosity raging, I pulled the top off at least thirty more boxes. After I had checked twenty-five boxes, I finally found gold coins from a different year coin —1898.

The boxes of coins were all arranged in order by date. I walked to the farthest end of the room to the last box, which should have contained the oldest coins and looked inside. The last box also contained the same $20 gold coins as I had just seen, and they were also from 1898. I could not know for sure how many coins were packed into the boxes in that room, but there were millions of them. Each one of those coins was probably worth over a thousand dollars, so there could be billions of dollars worth of gold coins in that room.

And Mike said there were lots of rooms like this. My head was reeling at the value of the treasure the Sasquatch had gathered.

8

For the next fifteen days, Mike took me to hundreds of caves to identify objects. At most of the caves, I only had a few things to identify, and at a few, I looked at objects for an hour or two. We were so busy I had only seen Daru once during the day, and that was fourteen days earlier. I missed being around her. Daru was always nice to me, and I owed her my gratitude for saving my life.

It was still spring, and the nights were cold and having a seven-foot-tall heater to keep me warm under the ferns and branches was nice. Although, as she was shedding her hair, it wouldn't have been as warm if she had been around.

One day we were in a cave where I had been asked to identify some items when I heard a familiar voice. That was Daru talking to Mike! I quickly turned around and gave her a big smile. She noticed how happy I was to see her, and Daru smiled back at me.

Daru spoke to Mike in Sasquatch for a few minutes. Mike had been working with me on learning Sasquatch all day as we worked for the last fifteen days, and I was starting to understand some of what was being said. I wanted to be able to communicate with Daru in Sasquatch and understand what was being said around me.

I had been kept so busy for the past couple of months I hadn't thought much about Daru. Now I noticed that she had shed her light fur even further. I was standing about twenty-five feet from Mike and Daru. Daru is seven feet tall, and Mike is just over five feet tall, so I chuckled at the contrast. Daru looked like a mother talking to her son —a stocky son with a full beard.

Wow, she's beautiful! I was no longer seeing Daru as an animal—a creature—but just as a beautiful human being. Her skin was a warm tan color and looked soft. With all her facial hair gone, for the first time, I could see her strong but attractive nose and high cheekbones without the fur covering. So beautiful. Mike had been correct, I was singing another tune when I saw Daru without hair.

I walked over to where Mike and Daru were talking with another huge smile on my face.

I could see she was smiling back at me. In Sasquatch, I said, "I am glad to see you again."

Daru looked surprised and said in her language, "I am impressed at how quickly you have learned my language." She went on to tell me how helpful my work was in identifying the items I had worked with over the last fifteen days.

Daru said, "My teachers are surprised humans have so many different cellphone designs." Apparently, the Sasquatch figure out the best of everything and make that the only option. They only had one phone design rather than having thousands of different ones like humans do.

We went on talking about how many of the other items I had helped with would be used to shed new light on the advancements humans had been making in electronics over the last twenty years. The satellite phones had surprised the Sasquatch, as did the GPS. Daru said, "We have waited many generations for humans to advance to this level and it is exciting to live through it."

Daru told me, "I feel happy you are doing so well. Is there anything you need to make your life more comfortable?"

"I'd like to see you more, as you are so nice to me."

Daru looked at me and gently ruffled my hair and said, "I'll make sure I am around more."

I awoke an hour after I had gone to bed that night. As she had before, Daru was snuggling against my back and holding me like a child. As her long, lean arms wrapped around me, I could feel warm skin now instead of warm, soft fur. She was like a mother hen keeping her baby chick warm.

* * *

One day while I was working away at inspecting items that needed to be identified, Daru came in to talk to me. She said, "You know Mike was speaking the truth when he said you can never go back to your old life, or at least not yet," she said.

"What does that mean?"

"Doug, you are the first human we have rescued in many years. We stopped years ago for fear we would get found while searching for lost or hurt humans. It was my luck I found you."

Then Daru lowered her head, a sad look crossing her face. She closed her eyes and was silent.

Is she praying? I wondered. I sat silent and unmoving for the next five minutes as she kept her head bowed.

I thought about a time when I had woken up later than usual and wondered if I'd get in trouble for missing work. Maybe Daru was like my boss and could excuse my absence. I had thought back on what had happened over the last few months, and a feeling of contentment had come over me. I knew these months had been the happiest time in my life.

Daru hadn't been around, so I got up and cleaned myself in the bathing corner. Most large caves had a corner that held a slightly concealed stream of running water for bathing. Once you got used to the chilly water, it felt great. Well, a nice hot shower would have really been nice.

In the area where the water drained, you would take care of your toilet business. The water washed the business out into a small river and underground. I have never asked how this worked, but now I suspect the Sasquatch built it to look like a natural setting. It must be highly advanced because each cave has a separate unit with a recycling water treatment system.

By the time I found Daru, she was deep in conversation with a human I had never met. This human was writing on a flat piece of what looked like rock with a flat smooth surface like a blackboard on one side. I was still staring at what looked like a writing slate when Daru introduced me to the new human.

"My name is Nancy," she said. She looked about sixty years old but was in great shape. Nancy started sharing her story. She said she did research and kept records for the Sasquatch.

"They found me hurt in the woods. I had been walking from one train rail car to another when I tripped and fell off the train going from Seattle to Tacoma."

"Did the Sasquatch find you in Renton?" I asked.

"What is Renton?"

Surprised she didn't know, I said, "Renton is a city between Seattle and Tacoma."

"Oh, never heard of it. That was the first train I had ever been on."

"Where did you board the train?"

"I was in downtown Seattle that year. I was thirty-five."

"When was that?"

"Let's see, that must have been in 1887, a long time ago."

When Nancy saw that I was speechless, she said, "Yes, Doug, I am 160 years old. But no, I am not the oldest human living with the Sasquatch. I have only aged about twenty-five years in the last 125 years, but I guarantee I am fitter than any sixty-year-old you have met."

"I don't doubt it," I said, still trying to decide if I should believe Nancy. Daru had left while we had been talking, so I thought I'd use the time alone with Nancy to learn all I could from her about living with the Sasquatch. We talked for the next few hours and even went outside and picked lunch together.

While I was recovering with Daru, someone else had picked our meals for us. Now I was picking my own meals again. It had been nice while it lasted, but I really didn't mind picking my own food. It helped the days go by and I could practice the Sasquatch language with others.

That day Nancy and I walked along a well-tended trail running parallel to the main trail and picked. It really was convenient to walk outside and pick up my meals. Other times, during the days when I was working in the caves, someone would bring baskets of hard-boiled eggs and raw eggs, as well as raw and cooked fish. I had never seen who placed the baskets of food and hadn't found out where they came from. I just knew I was grateful to have something more than greens and berries.

While we browsed for our lunch, Nancy told me about her time with the Sasquatch. Nancy told of the gentleness of the Sasquatch and the love they feel for all creatures. She spoke of when the Sasquatch found her and took her in. Many more humans were working with the Sasquatch back then. "The Sasquatch were not worried about humans back then like they are now," she said. For the past thirty years, the Sasquatch had stayed away from humans and kept any sign of themselves well hidden.

"Of course," Nancy said, "the technology that made the tree camouflage for the doors can work as a camouflage for all the other signs of Sasquatch civilization."

"Like what?"

"Oh, Sasquatch trails near homes, towns, and even a trail in a Seattle park."

I imagined how easy it was for the Sasquatch to make a door look like a tree, so why not make a trail look like a rock wall? The possibilities for their technology were tantalizing and unlimited.

After my time with Nancy, which I had enjoyed, I began feeling calm and even a bit excited about what my life from here on could be. But a troubling thought remained lodged in my mind, would I be destined to be with the Sasquatch forever, like Nancy?

9

I t was around the first part of July, almost four months since I had been taken in by the Sasquatch. There was talk of winter setting in. I had fallen into the river in March and was immobile for six weeks. The last seven weeks I had gone from one cave system to another with Mike and Daru to identify items. Along the way, I had met a few nice human captives like Nancy.

Winter set in early here in the mountains. The trails the Sasquatch used were all over four thousand feet above sea level or more. The first snow would close all trails and that snow could fall up here as early as September or October.

I wondered what the winters would be like with the Sasquatch. Did the Sasquatch hibernate in the winter? That didn't sound like such a bad idea with the cold. Or did they go to a lower elevation to get away from the snow?

I heard Daru call my name. "Doug, come. Would you like to see some beautiful sights?"

Daru and I walked from cave to cave over the next few days as she told me the history of her kind and how they have watched over humans as they have evolved for the past three million years. The Sasquatch had only held their current level of technology for over three-and-a-half million years and had been to space. Some of them still live in space close to Earth and beyond, but most enjoy the simple lifestyle in the forests.

Daru said Sasquatch live all over the world, especially where there is an abundance of trees, but the area from California into Canada along the Cascade Mountains is their favorite home. With a smile, she talked of the white Sasquatch on the other side of the world who chose to live in a very primitive way and not eat animal flesh.

"Are you talking about the Yeti?"

"Yes, that is them. I could not live like that," she said. "I like to take a bath occasionally."

With that said, Daru grabbed me and began undressing me. I was about as effective at stopping this incredibly strong woman from taking my clothes off as a five-year-old would be against his mom.

In short order, I was undressed and being carried over the shoulder of a seven-foot-tall woman. Daru had been able to hold me down and strip me like I was a baby, carry me like a sack of potatoes, and now I was sure I had a bath coming.

We came to a small pool that looked dark, as if it was deep and cold. Sasquatches are less affected by cold temperatures than humans, so an ice-cold river or pool makes a fine bath. I usually prefer the warmer water of the caves for my bath, but Daru had other ideas of comfort.

She began to lift me over her head. I weighed about 275 pounds, although I had slimmed down some on my present diet of mostly greens. Daru had no trouble pressing me above her head as if I were nothing. Suddenly she squatted down, jumped straight up, and tossed me. I must have flown fifteen feet before I hit the water. I dreaded the shock of the ice-cold water coming, but when I hit with a huge splash, a pleasant feeling of warmth surrounded me as I sank to the bottom of the pool and sputtered my way up. The water was warm, not freezing cold.

The water was a perfect depth to bathe in without drowning if you are a Sasquatch who doesn't swim. I wiped the water out of my eyes and saw Daru grinning at me.

"Thank you for the nice warm surprise," I said.

"You are welcome."

"Can I give you a surprise?" I asked. When Daru smiled and nodded yes, I grabbed her without warning and managed to pick her up. We fell over in the water together, and Daru got totally soaked. Sasquatch cannot swim and really don't like getting their heads wet. It was time to show this strong woman that brains can beat brawn, and getting her head wet was the best way to show her that. I released her as soon as we hit the water so she would not be scared. She stood up quickly and shook off the water from her head. She then gave me her I-am-going-to-bite-you look then smiled and smiled.

We stayed near the pool for the next two days relaxing and enjoying the warm water, eating from the forest during the day, and at night making beds of grass, ferns, and leaves. I felt as if I could stay right there in that beautiful place forever.

On the morning of the third day, Daru told me, "It is time to go." The Sasquatch life is extremely simple. They have no bills, taxes, cars, or any other annoying and time-consuming things. Most Sasquatch carry little when they travel. They have their own clothes built-in, and food and lodging are easy and free.

But I wore clothes during the daytime and carried a small pack. Inside were things I thought I would need and warm clothes for the coming winter of rain and snow.

The Sasquatch do not talk much when they travel. After my first days traveling, right after I was healed, I wondered if they were even able to talk because they had been so quiet. Daru could talk for hours sitting, foraging, or in our bed nest, but she would go for hours straight without saying a word if we were walking. As soon as we stopped, she'd start right up again. I wondered if the silent walking tradition was left over from days when Sasquatch had predators—the last few thousand years since man has had weapons that could hurt an unsuspecting Sasquatch.

Once when we had stopped to browse for lunch, Daru began

talking about how sad it was that intelligent beings like humans would kill for sport or just because they were scared. Daru said she knew of stories about Sasquatch being shot. Surprisingly, she said none had died by human hands in the thousands of years humans have wielded weapons. Her face looked sad, so I stood closer to her while we finished lunch.

With many days left to travel, we could not spend any more time there. After lunch, we began walking again. Daru seemed to want to talk. Daru spent the next three weeks as we walked, telling me about the Sasquatch. We rarely spoke English, saving the English for at night in bed.

"You may be right, Doug, about the old memories and walking silently. We travel often and we lose many hours of communicating each day. I must speak with the elders about this matter. To you, it seems simple; to us, it has been the same for millions of years and worked—so why change it? Our mission is balance and harmony with all things. But that was formalized back when we had to worry about being eaten."

I learned about the Sasquatch farm on a global scale. They plant foods they like and need to survive through the area surrounding the corridor they live and work in. They have hundreds of distinct hybrid species of plant. Some groups that gather food for storage consist of both Sasquatch and humans together. Daru said we would meet many of the humans during the winter. Many of the humans like to work in the big communities rather than walk all over the mountains.

I spoke up and said, "I'm fine staying outside. I've got some winter clothes to keep myself warm outside even this winter."

"Don't worry about getting cold this winter, Doug."

"Why not? I do worry. I can't grow thicker hair. I will always need warm clothes to go outside."

Daru laughed, saying, "Doug, we will spend many moon cycles in the social units around this range."

"Social units?"

"Yes, social units mean small towns in English."

"If there are small towns in the woods, why have humans not discovered them?" I asked.

Daru smiled and said, "These towns are all underground and are nice and warm even on the coldest snowy days outside."

How on earth could the Sasquatch have built towns underground? I wondered.

"Remember, the Sasquatch have been living in this area for millions of years," Daru said.

"Hmm," I said, and then wondered aloud if a single Sasquatch using a shovel were to dig for that period, would it have been able to build one such social unit?

"Ah, but Doug, digging by hand is not needed with our technology," Daru said. "We grow our tunnels and rooms, as well as the doors and many other items we use."

"Grow? What do you mean by grow?"

"We have a way to turn the stone and dirt into a liquid, and then it is heated and formed by energy waves."

I just stared at her, wondering what bizarre thing I was going to hear next.

"If we have a need for a cave or tunnel, it is talked about. If the need is decided to be of value, then a troop goes to the spot and measures where and how it should be built. Once the decision is made, we use an electric tool that sends a beam into the rock at just the strength and depth to liquefy the needed area. Then the tool uses an energy pulse that acts like a balloon being blown up inside the liquid stone and dirt. The beam makes a tube or room of any size needed by pushing the liquid to the side, and then the tool heats the liquid that has been pushed aside. Once the liquid is heated, it turns into a glass-like substance that is stronger than diamonds."

Amazed by Daru's story, I wanted more information. "How big can a room be made?"

"I am sure there is no limit. I have seen pictures of your sports stadiums and biggest buildings and believe they can build rooms that big at least. We have many towns under many mountains. There are over seven million Sasquatch throughout the world currently, and almost one million live on this very mountain range spread out from northern Canada to Mexico. Until 500 years ago, this was an empty place and we Sasquatch had free range of this state. No one knows for sure how many are in space because they have been quieter since humans have developed space flight."

Daru was just getting warmed up. "My people spend more time underground these days because of humans. We are amazingly comfortable. Each town is self-sufficient and self-sustaining. Doug, my people have been building caves this way and have lived this exact way for two-and-one-half million years with hardly a change. Natural disasters like earthquakes, volcanic activity, and even asteroids and comets can cause the Sasquatch trouble and make us move, but mostly we try to keep things the same. We do so without hurting anyone or anything. We live to do no harm."

"But don't you like things to change once in a while . . . for the fun of it?"

"I see how you could think never changing doesn't bring as much joy as trying something new." Daru was silent for a good while before she looked at me with her light green eyes and said, "Doug, you humans scare the Sasquatch. You humans have changed more in the last one hundred years than we have changed in two and one half million years. We fear you will outpace our technology and pass us by within the next couple of hundred years. Then we will no longer be safely hidden from your kind."

The thought that humans would hurt Daru because she was different made me sick. "What can I do to help?"

"You are helping, Doug. You are helping us understand the humans and their technology so we can make better choices about our future."

After we had walked through some rugged terrain for some time, I asked Daru, "What do some of the other humans do?"

"Oh, the humans make great food gatherers because they can get into berry bushes easier. Even simple plant gathering is easier because humans are shorter and do not have to bend as much. They are not afraid of water, so they are better fishermen.

"We have many of our staple plants that we grow to higher heights for ease of picking, but many of the wild plants are low, and again, humans really help. We have done such an excellent job with farming and using special hybrids that picking is easy and does not take much time for each social unit.

"The Sasquatch ideal is that no one has to work too hard or too long and that everyone has the time to study, explore, play, investigate or do anything they choose to do if it does not hurt a being or the earth. Humans are smaller with more nimble bodies and so do less damage to the surrounding forest while gathering food, so they were prized, treated with great appreciation, and all care is taken to assure they did not overwork."

One thing I knew for sure was that humans could not escape. We were, in fact, prisoners, but not slaves. No one was made to work. You could lay in bed all day, go outside to eat, and go back to bed. No one judged another for what they did or did not do. The Sasquatch were always appreciative when you contributed.

The Sasquatch also liked humans for being able to assemble small parts. The Sasquatch developed their science and tailored items they use for their size, but at times a human's smaller size beat their technology.

Daru had told me about a time many years earlier when a Sasquatch dropped a large gemstone the size of an egg and it rolled into a wall vent. One of the children in the room ran to the wall, crawled into the tube and a few seconds later came crawling out with the stone in her teeth. That little girl saved many hours of time, as the Sasquatch would have had to get equipment that could probe down the tube. So she got to keep the gemstone as thanks.

It is just easier for a human to work in confined spaces on plumbing, which the Sasquatch put between the walls. I was surprised to learn that Sasquatch used humans as surgeons and valued artists and musicians. They had not spent much time or effort in producing art and music, striving instead to live in peace and quiet. Music was not part of their culture until humans introduced it. Now to their credit, many Sasquatch like music, and a few were learning to appreciate art.

Each human with them has the right to choose their work and can change jobs. Mostly the jobs are to keep people busy so they feel productive, but many of the jobs the humans do make life easier for all, and the humans feel they are appreciated. No one is required to work more than three hours a day. The only requirement for Sasquatch and humans is that everyone must browse for most of their meals when outside or around the cave systems. In towns, they can go outside and browse but also eat in the indoor gardens or in a place much like a salad bar, only bigger. They do not eat meat except fish and eggs.

Most of the humans I've met say they love living with the Sasquatch and do not want to leave and return to their old homes. Many of them had been with the Sasquatch for thirty to 150 years and would not know what to do if they went back. Their families had long passed away, and there was nothing left to go back to.

But I have talked in private with many other humans and there were a few who had never wanted to stay. They liked the Sasquatch but hated being prisoners. A few who had been with the Sasquatch for over one hundred years still wanted to go back, if for no other reason than to be free.

I keep this a secret, but that's the way I feel. As the days went by, each morning when I awoke, I thought first about getting away to see my mother. *If I could just let her know I am alive*, I think in the quiet of the early mornings. Mother would be sick with worry. Would she come to the conclusion that I am dead and my body is lost in the Cascades Mountains somewhere? Is she suffering great pain from my loss?

The more I think about my mother, the worse I feel. I like living with the Sasquatch and Daru is a great friend and teacher. I don't want to leave. I only wish my mother could be brought to see me if I can't go to her.

I have been with the Sasquatch for over four months and now my main goal has come to be finding a way to let my mother know I am alive. It was only the two of us in our little family as Mother is my only living relative. There is no one else.

They'll never let me go to see my mother. I knew this to be true at my core. The thought makes me so sad I can't hide it. Sometimes I see Daru looking at me, wondering what's wrong. Then she comes to me, wraps her arms around me, and holds me tightly. When I try to tell Daru what I am feeling, she listens.

One time, I said aloud, "I want to see my mother."

She responded, "I am very sorry you are so sad, Doug. I wish there were something I could do to help. But it is forbidden."

Maybe it was that word "forbidden." Or maybe I just had to try before I gave up. I began to think about how I could get a message to my mother.

I was writing in this notebook one day when I hatched up this plan. I would send a message saying I need rescuing. If I include my diary and some gold coins, it is possible someone would help . . . if they found it.

My plan was made. Now I am waiting for the right place and time to implement it.

10

I finished reading the diary to complete silence. No one moved for a full minute before I broke the silence. I looked at the group and asked, "Does anyone still want to help look for Doug?"

Bill was the first to speak. "You bet I want to go," he said, "but I won't be going without protection."

"Oh, come on, you do not plan to kill them, do you?" I asked.

"No way, Matt! Those Sasquatch are worth too much to science alive to kill them. I was planning to bring tranquilizer guns along to do what we need to do without hurting them. If those things are as big as Doug says, then we need to be armed, but no, we do not have to kill. They seem strong as hell but peaceful."

Bill looked around the room at his employees and asked, "Is there anyone here who does not want to come along? If you choose not to come, you can stay here. I promise you will still get a full share."

One guy raised his hand and another sitting next to him did as well. The first guy said, "Hey Bill, Joe and I want to help, but maybe it'd be smarter if we stay back in the equipment van as backup. Not because we are both scared." The looks on their faces told a different story.

"No sweat Gus, we needed a couple guys to do just that. Those jobs are yours. Anyone else want to stay back?"

No one else spoke up, and Bill said, "Just as I thought, you are all nuts—and great scientists too."

The room broke out into some noisy, excited conversations for a few minutes until Bill called for silence. "OK, Matt, looks like you have a rescue crew. Now it is up to you to lead us to the spot."

Someone from the back of the room said, "I've got an idea about that."

"What is it, Terry?" asked Bill.

"I was thinking, why use hand-drawn maps when we have access to a state-of-the-art satellite."

"Clever idea, if that thing can get close enough for our needs."

Terry said, "My girl can see a peanut you drop on the sidewalk, so I think she can find a well-used trail."

Bill bowed and said, "Sorry for saying your girl is not good enough for this. Hope I didn't hurt your feelings. Now go fire up that girl of yours and let's see if you can find that spot Matt is talking about."

Terry nearly sprinted out of the room, and the lab guys moved in that direction. Bill put one arm around my shoulder while we were following the guys and said, "Matt, you are one great guy. Offering to share the wealth is beyond amazing. These guys are poor scientists and would have worked for just the glory. Your generous offer has given them something they never dreamed of—a chance to be rich and famous, or at least not have to worry about bills anymore, and for a greater career than they had hoped for."

"No sweat, Bill. There is enough here for everyone already and I expect we will be seeing much more in the future."

"I just can't get over your generosity, Matt. You're as good a human as you are a runner." He slapped me on the back and said, "Let's see if Terry's girl can find that cliff of yours."

"Terry's girlfriend works here?"

Bill laughed and said, "Terry doesn't get out much, so we call his computer his girlfriend. So don't say anything unkind about computers or critique the search he is doing, or his feelings will be hurt." He laughed again. "Sometimes he acts like it *is* his girlfriend. Sounds like a scientist thing, doesn't it? Actually, Terry is the best computer guy we have and the system he is working on has helped us with tracking game.

"The military has access to everything we look at and how Terry gathers the information using the satellite. By changing the satellite configuration in ways no one has before, Terry is able to see things no one has been able to see using a satellite. Looking over Terry's shoulder has helped the military use these satellites to locate bad guys even in rough tree-covered terrain. So, if we have Terry, we have use of that satellite. I'm not able to pay him what he deserves here, but he gets to play with the satellite, so I don't worry about him leaving, at least for now."

Terry was at his computer terminal, ready to go. He looked at me and said, "OK, Matt, what part of the Cascades were you in?

"Just off I-90 after milepost 105. You take the Stampede Pass Highway, exit south and head up to Lost Lake. Terry punched in a few commands and the screen started shifting. As he did, he muttered, "Come on, girl."

I just smiled and saw what Bill had been saying. While entering commands, Terry said, "The lab has access to this government satellite in exchange for helping them occasionally with a difficult search and allowing the government in on how I use the satellite."

Bill jumped in, saying, "We've done many jobs over the years for Washington State and the US government, and in exchange, the lab gets to use the satellite to watch various herds migrate."

Terry added, "If we stay away from restricted military bases, we have unrestricted use."

I stared at the screen, thinking how much easier that satellite would have made looking for a good mountain running spot than driving around for months like I did to find the road that eventually led me to the backpack and diary.

"I'm getting close, so you might want to step in and guide me the rest of the way." Terry glanced at me.

As I stepped closer to the monitor, I was amazed. I had zoomed in with Google Maps, but it never looked this clear, and it was never in real-time. I could see a car driving on a dirt road by Lost Lake. "Too cool, Terry," I said.

"Yes, my girl is sweet, is she not?"

"Let me look for a second and get my bearings." The resolution was so good it only took a few seconds for me to find the road that met up with the washed-out bridge. "You see that small road to the right? Follow that until you see a river. Terry punched in more commands, and the scene moved until I could see a river and what was left of the washed-out bridge.

"There's the bridge. Can you pull the view back so I can see the whole twenty-five-mile loop?"

"Sure." Terry zoomed out so we could see the area around the mountain loop I had been running.

I looked at the screen for a minute until I got my bearings. Once I was sure of the spot, I said, "That's the spot, Terry."

Terry nodded and again, he quickly zoomed in to where I was pointing. When the zoom stopped, I could see the cliff as if I were standing right there.

"That's the cliff," I said. "That's the spot where I found the diary in the pack!"

Terry shifted the view up, so I could easily recognize the top of the cliff and the tree I leaned against to read the diary.

"Oh man, Terry, your girl is a good looker!"

Terry gave me a big smile and said, "And she never complains either."

I looked at the new image and said, "There's the trail."

Bill looked over my shoulder and said, "Follow that trail to the right for a while."

As the screen panned to the right, it was easy to see a well-worn trail just below the ridge line.

"Sure looks like a game trail," said Terry, "except for one thing." He zoomed in closer, pointed to the trail, and said, "It's too big for a normal game trail. Whatever travels that trail has also made improvements that do not happen in nature. You can tell by the work around the rockslides and small creeks."

"Nice catch Terry," said Bill, "which is why you are the computer man."

"I'll follow the trail in both directions as far as I can and let you know what I find." The detail was so sharp that Terry could zoom in on the smallest of rocks on the path.

We left Terry to work and I followed Bill to a storeroom at the back of the building. Bill stopped at a group of shelves near the back and said, "You may want to check this out, Matt." The shelves were full of electronic equipment, including tasers and thermal imaging equipment. The rest I couldn't identify, but it looked complicated and expensive.

Bill smiled at the look on my face and said, "We collect big boy toys. We have enough equipment here to find and follow anything that lives in the woods. Terry will map out the trail for us using the satellite. Once we have the layout, we can plan where to place the forward scouts and cameras so we can see anything coming from as far away as possible.

"I'd like to have at least twenty-four hours' notice before we encounter those Sasquatch. From what Doug says in the diary, they are as smart as humans, and they are big. That gives them the advantage in most areas. If we can tranquilize all or most of them before they know we are even there, we'll have a chance to rescue Doug. My plan is to use all this equipment to its fullest extent," Bill said.

"Do you know what to do with all this stuff?"

"No worries. Each of my guys can shoot a tranquilizer gun like a pro. If we take them by surprise, we can pull it off without a hitch. But otherwise, we may be in for a hard fight with a tough foe. These tranquilizer guns are a bit different than most. They are not single-shot guns like the normal ones. My lab guys engineered them here, each gun can shoot six shots like a revolver."

"Six shots! We don't want to kill them."

"No, these will only knock out the prey; they won't kill them," said Bill. "Listen, I've figured it out. I will have ten men total. Two will stay in the van and monitor the radios, transport needed equipment up to us and act as a safety backup if needed. Six of us will be at the base camp right off the trail near where you found the pack and we will each have these guns. I also want to send two men further up the trail with the hope of spotting the Sasquatch as they are traveling. I would guess we can find a spot further up the trail to give us at least twenty-four hours' notice before they reach our position."

Bill was on a roll and seemed excited about the planning. He said, "Matt, you won't need to carry a tranquilizer gun unless you want to. According to the diary, the troop Doug travels with only has eight Sasquatch. The six of us from the lab should be able to take them down with ease. I will be making up a special tranquilizer based on the specific size and chemistry of the Sasquatch. We know they are like us, so the drug should be a simple one to make. I promise you it will not harm them, but it will need to be strong so it can work within a few seconds."

"Oh, heck, Bill," I said, "I might want one of those guns for myself. If I am in the woods with big powerful hairy things, I want a chance to protect myself."

Bill smiled, "Don't worry, we'll get you something. But you may need some instruction on how to use it, including what to do if you shoot yourself," and he laughed.

I ignored Bill's last comment, not finding it quite as funny as he did. I said, "Well, I see you've got the equipment and personnel I need to find and track Doug and the Sasquatch, but let's talk timing. How soon can you leave? We know they travel from May through September, and it's already the first part of July. That means we only have two months to find them and rescue Doug."

"That's not a problem," said Bill. "In our line of work, we have to be flexible and ready to leave in a matter of hours to follow a herd once it is spotted. Business is slow right now, and we can offload anything that needs to get done sooner to one of our competitors. Most of the guys working at the lab are unmarried or in a relationship. They're scientists and they are married to their work."

That remark hit the target with me and I said, "Same for most of the top runners I know."

Bill said, "How about if I work toward getting everything ready to go by Saturday?"

"That's pretty quick, but it would work for me. Running is my job, and I don't have a pet or girlfriend, so I can be ready by Saturday. I'll meet with the coin dealer on Friday, then I am free."

"So, Bill, what do I need to bring?"

"Just bring what you need to stay in the woods for a few weeks to a month. We will supply the regular food, and you can bring anything special you need."

"I won't need much except the high-calorie stuff I carry when I am running and my hydration pack. I'll pick up some special trail running shoes while I am thinking about it. The rocks on mountain trails can be brutal on the feet with normal running shoes."

"Stay connected if something comes up. Otherwise, I will see you Saturday morning here at the lab. It's going to be a great adventure," Bill said as he walked me to the door.

I tried to lower his expectations a little and said, "It might not all be great, and we might not find any Sasquatch, but I at least want to try to help this guy out."

11

I t was Tuesday, so I had a few days to pick up the things I needed
for the trip. My first stop was at REI for new trail running shoes.
It was time to get a bigger hammock as well. There was no way I was
going to sleep on the ground up there with Sasquatch walking
around. Doug had written that the Sasquatch do not climb, so I
planned to stay above ground out of their hairy reach. I would get a
good rope ladder. Climbing up trees is hard work, and a nice ladder
would make getting up or down much easier. A couple of extra headlamps and batteries were on the list as I thought about climbs
needing to be made in the dark. Maybe I'd look at a Lug-A-Loo so I
wouldn't have to leave the tree to do my business.

If I had to pack it myself, I'd nix that. But the lab guys would be
using an electric cart to move most of our gear from the cars to base
camp. I didn't have any money worries now, so I could buy what I
needed and wanted without worrying about cash for the first time in
a long time. I thought I'd pay my bills a month or two in advance
while I was at it.

That night I came home with a new deluxe hard-bottomed tree
hammock the size of a large tent, a seventy-five-foot lightweight rope
ladder, three pairs of new trail running shoes, and two headlamps

with extra batteries. At the running store, I bought enough energy bars and goo packets to live on for a month. I figured I could get in quite a bit of trail running while we waited for Doug and the troop to show. I average an energy goo packet every five miles, so I needed a bunch to last me a whole month.

All I had to do before I left was meet Randy to see what he found out about the coins. This adventure was getting exciting. But then I remembered the feeling I had when I left the mountain a few days ago. Part of me did not want to ever go back up to the mountain because I was scared. Part of me was excited because this was the most momentous thing to happen to me in all my life. All I ever did was run. I wasn't a risk taker as I always worried about hurting myself, so I had missed exciting or risky endeavors—and here I was, getting ready to hunt Sasquatch. I knew I wouldn't dare look for Doug without Bill and his well-equipped crew. It looked like I was making up for a life lacking in excitement in one shot.

* * *

On Thursday, I headed down to the lab to drop my bulky stuff off to be loaded onto the trucks for the Saturday departure. Bill wanted my gear on a truck, even if I was going to drive my own van, so they could know the full weight and keep stuff organized.

At the lab, I saw most of the machines and equipment were turned off, and the lab was all but shut down. They were still running more tests on the hair samples on the few remaining running machines. Bill told me they were going to continue testing and retesting for various things.

Bill waved me over and said, "I spent most of last night writing a report with the information we have gathered about the Sasquatch from the hair samples." He said he was sending it all to a lab in DC owned by his friend. That lab would retest to see if they got the same results as a double check.

Bill and I went to the back of the lab, where a small group was clustered around a pair of weird bikes. I saw some guys working on their own projects, which I assumed were for our rescue mission, but Bill wanted to show me the bikes.

He said, "These two ugly bicycles could kick my ass on any twenty-mile mountain run. They have a thirty-five-mile-per-hour top speed going uphill, can go fifty miles on a charge at top speed, and boy, can they climb hills."

I looked at him and then the two bikes and shook my head. "Honestly? Can they really go thirty-five mph?"

"Yup. And with the flexible solar panel rolled up and stored in the handlebars, they can fully recharge in two hours and be ready for another fifty miles. The biggest advantage these bikes have, aside from the electric power, is that they are two-wheel drive, so they can really fly in sand, snow, or loose uphill roads."

"I could really use one of these to scout my running roads—that is, unless I can use that satellite map system," I said.

Bill snorted and said, "Fat chance on both of those dreams. The bike is a top-secret prototype we are testing for the army—and the map system is so not going to happen. He grinned and said, "Although, if you happened to come by for lunch occasionally and we are looking at game trails, you might find a perfect trail for training."

It felt good to be accepted as a member of the team around here —I felt like I was back on a college team again.

I think the feeling went both ways as Bill said, "Look, Matt, you've made every one of us in this lab feel alive by letting us join on this rescue. I am sure you feel a bit safer as well."

"For sure. I couldn't do this by myself."

"Matt, we all thank you from the bottom of our hearts for this opportunity. Even if we never find a living Sasquatch, our lab studies on the hair will put this lab and all the scientists working here on the cover of every science journal and magazine. This means the world to our careers, and we truly thank you. And besides, it makes us feel like our lives mean something."

There was a moment where no one spoke, then there was a lot of back-slapping and handshaking for a few minutes until Bill asked for silence.

"Alright, listen up. We've all completed our assigned tasks, so we are now ready to attempt this rescue. On the way, we hope to gather as much scientific information as we can. If we do get a Sasquatch, rescue Doug, and get more of that treasure, then we can add even more to our resumes and contribute to the advancement of science.

"OK, let's talk details. We will have the trucks completely loaded by tomorrow afternoon. Take time today to finish any last-minute details at home before leaving. Remember, this excursion could last for over a month, so make sure that you have everything taken care of for at least that amount of time. Again, do I need to remind you that you are not to disclose any of this to anyone outside this circle?"

The serious looks on the guys' faces and little headshakes gave the correct answer, and Bill resumed his instructions. "As with all missions we have done in the past, there will be a few individuals back here at the lab who know what we are doing. We'll stay in contact with them and relay all data we gather back here to them. They are our final backup if anything happens. Meet back here at the lab at 7:00 a.m. Saturday."

As the guys began to disperse, Bill said, "Thank you, again."

I shook his hand and said, "This is like the science Olympics to you and your lab guys, isn't it? You all have a chance to make your mark. I'm glad we can do this as a team. I wouldn't want to do this alone."

Bill and I walked out to the trucks in the back as he wanted to show me all the special equipment they were bringing.

I thought, *more equipment*? I said, "It's five or six miles from the washed-out bridge and the cliff, so bringing all this stuff is going to take a lot of bike trips. We might need more of those bikes to haul everything."

He motioned me over to his side as he walked up to a box trailer, opened the door and walked in. The inside of that trailer looked like a race car garage, except, instead of cars, they had eight ATVs inside. All eight were identical: 350 cc, four-wheel drive with a front and rear winch. I looked at Bill and said, "They might do the trick except for one thing."

"What's that?"

"The bridge is out."

"No problem," he said. "We are putting up a portable cable car that will span the river and easily hold one of the ATVs at a time. Joe and Gus will stay with the trucks with the remainder of the gear. We need one ATV at base camp for them, so we could let you use the remaining one if you decide not to run. Remember, we can carry all your gear, so it is not a big deal either way.

"Sounds great."

Bill said, "It's a good thing Joe and Gus decided to stay."

"Yeah? Why?"

"We'll need to communicate with the lab computers so they can monitor that as needed. Our safety protocols require that we have at least two people behind for safety. Besides, the gear we will be leaving behind is too valuable to be left unattended."

"You're right. You know Bill, I may take you up on the offer of that ATV. Once at our camp, I can do my runs and save my energy for better running trails higher up the mountain. I may even run the suspected Sasquatch trail and see what I can find. If I use an ATV, I can bring a bit more gear for comfort and better running."

"That'll work. I'll have our two guys on bikes go out thirty-five miles from our base camp on Friday and see what they can see, but having your third set of eyes could really help, especially going slower than my two bike-crazy techs will."

The last thing Bill showed me was a fancy zip line. Bill said, "The military tested this high-tech zip line for an emergency escape route for use in the mountains of Afghanistan. It was super light and could run for up to a half mile long. You could put one on your tree in case you want to get down in a hurry."

"Not a bad idea, considering the Sasquatch did not climb. We could all escape in an emergency."

Bill laughed, "I'm hoping there won't be that kind of an emergency. My guys could drop twenty charging Sasquatch in a few moments with their tranquilizer guns, so we probably won't need it. But you can have one yourself, just to be sure."

I just laughed, as if it was no big deal, but thought, *I'm putting one of those zip lines on my tree and down the mountainside.* Even if I didn't need it to escape, a half-mile zip line slide would be just plain fun. There was no way I wanted to be trapped in a tree with a huge hairy ape looking up at me.

The plan was there were going to be eleven of us on the rescue mission—Bill, his nine lab partners, and me. Eleven people against an unknown number of Sasquatch sounded risky. Was I really ready for this? Bill and his people were going in their three trucks, and I was leading them to the spot driving my own van. The two bikers, Steve and Lou, were heading out early Friday morning, so they could be comfortably settled into their spot thirty-five miles away by the time we reached our base camp. Bill told me that Terry and the bikers had traced the Sasquatch trail to the north, about thirty-five miles from where we would have the base camp near where I found the diary. They found an old, abandoned logging road that came within a few miles of the Sasquatch trail in that area. The bikers were going to use the smaller game trails from the road to intersect with the Sasquatch trail.

Once they reached the Sasquatch trail, they would set up a forward scout camp with 24-hour electronic monitoring equipment to look for and track the Sasquatch once they had been spotted. The equipment was all computerized and automatic, so the guys wouldn't need to monitor it. That would allow them to easily scout up and down the trail from their camp, looking for signs of Sasquatch.

Steve and Lou should be able to see the Sasquatch about fifty miles away from our main base camp. That would give us about two days' notice before the Sasquatch reach our base camp from the time they are spotted. They would only have a small amount of equipment they are going to be carrying on their bikes, but it would be more than enough to allow us to download and analyze all the data we need. Steve and Lou would then forward the data.

Bill told me, "I've assigned the lab techs each a different part of the data to analyze. I'm sorry I can't give you a task because it would take too long to train you, Matt. But I want to give you a laptop so you will be able to watch everything going on. We'll all be wearing special headsets with wireless mics, cameras, and a pair of glasses with a built-in heads-up display. This system can listen in on and see what everyone in our group sees and hears. Also, everyone else will be able to listen to you and see what you see. It even has a rear-view camera so you can see what is going on behind you. You can voice activate the system or use the icons on the display. I suggest you watch what you say or do, or these guys will have a great time laughing at your funny mistakes."

"Roger that," I said, getting in the spirit of the moment.

"Oh, and don't forget to take it off when you use the facilities."

I was still laughing when I walked away from Bill's, "See you Saturday morning."

12

I woke up Friday morning and headed out for my normal run on auto-pilot. When I hit the ten-mile mark of my twenty-mile run, I let myself think about the expedition ahead. *Am I in over my head going on the trip?* Bill and his guys were experienced in tracking and capturing wild animals. All I did well was run. *Maybe I can chase the Sasquatch down and capture Doug,* I thought, then laughed at that ridiculous thought. I am a not-so-tall distance runner, Doug is a six-foot, nine-inch giant, and he can't get away from the Sasquatch. *What am I thinking? How could I be of any help?*

One thing I did have in my favor, I knew the area like the back of my hand after running every square foot of the place.

After my run, I finished packing for the trip. I checked and double-checked my gear. It felt like I was going overseas for an important ultra-race. If I forgot anything for a 250-mile race, I could get hurt badly or even die, so with that on my mind, I triple-checked my gear. Satisfied I had not forgotten anything, I closed my bags and stowed the gear by the door for my early departure.

I grabbed a bite to eat and left for the bank to get the coins for my meeting with Randy at the coin shop, wondering on the way what he had found out. I decided to take the rest of the coins with me when I went to the shop. I would be out of town for a long time, and if Randy had a buyer, he'd need the coins. I wasn't sure if I should load him down with the responsibility of protecting the coins, but if he was going to sell them, he'd need instant access.

At the bank, I pulled the heavy safe deposit box out and set it on the table. Pulling the leather bag out, I looked inside. For just a second, I was afraid the bag would be empty and this was all a dream. Then I saw the glimmering coins. Satisfied that the coins were still in the bag, I opened one of the smaller bags, took out ten of the $20 dollar pieces, and put them back into the safe deposit box. The coins I put back were of a lower value and not rare, but if anything went wrong, I would still have enough money from those coins to last a while. I placed the bag into my backpack, replaced the safe-deposit box and left the bank.

The drive to Randy's coin shop made me nervous. All of Randy's talk about some coin collectors being above the law made me over-think everything. *What if the shop is closed down and Randy has taken the coins and run?* I tried to shake the thoughts from my mind as I drove to the shop.

When I walked in the door, Randy looked at the clock, smiled and said, "Hey, Matt, right on time. I figured you, of all people, would be prompt."

"Why is that?"

"You're a runner," said Randy. "Every runner I know is always on time. I've always wanted to ask one of you why and now I have my chance."

I laughed and said, "I'm not a good one to ask. I don't keep a very tight schedule at all. I don't have a job, so I don't have to be on time for anything except the finish line."

"Cute, Matt, cute," he said.

"Well, any news for me—good or bad?"

"I have news, and it's all good. I sold every coin you gave me. And the best news is I have buyers for all the rest if you still want to sell them all."

"Do I? Now that's a silly question to ask a guy who does not have a job."

Randy gave a chuckle, then said, "Whenever you want to bring more coins in, I will take them. You might be interested to know most of the coins are going to be bought by dealers."

"Oh? Why is that?"

"Well, we dealers pride ourselves on having a good personal collection. Your coins would be the best any of us have ever seen, and of course, we would like to have the first chance at buying them. I plan to buy more than a few of the best ones myself."

"Makes sense," I said. "You would have to be a big collector to start a coin shop."

"Right, Matt. I buy what I can and only sell the ones I do not want. The best part is all my dealer friends will be paying cash and want to keep it off the books. That means you won't have to pay tax on the proceeds. It also means you must keep the money out of sight, like in your safe- deposit box."

"You don't have to tell me twice, Randy."

"So just let me know when you want to start, and I will start peddling the wares."

"Well, right now, I have a problem with time."

"What do you mean?"

"I told you the story about the coins and the missing guy."

"Yes, and it is too weird to be true. If you hadn't brought me the coins, I would say you are nuts."

"Well, I took the hair samples to a lab, and the findings prove the story in the diary. Whatever is holding this guy Doug is not human and is not monkey, but a relative of both."

Randy was just staring at me with a look of disbelief, so I kept talking. "The lab guys want to help find Doug and the . . . well . . . let us call them Sasquatch. They specialize in tracking, capturing and DNA testing animals. After the tests came back, they wanted in on helping find and free Doug. They have all the high-tech equipment and gear to do the job. If we find any more coins, I'm going to split the profits with them."

"Whoa! Are you sure you want to do that?"

"Aw, I already have enough coins to satisfy my needs for a life-time, and I really need their help, so I offered them a deal. The deal is everyone gets an even split." I stopped talking for a moment, then said, "Including you, Randy."

Now Randy was just staring at me with a flat-out look of surprise, eyes wide, mouth open. I said, "The way I see it, all the lab guys, you, and I will split any more coins, treasure, or even fame equally. I mean that. You will have a heck of a job spreading these coins around and saving these guys from any hassles that could come from getting rid of the coins, so it's worth an even cut for you as well."

I reached over and gave Randy a couple of pats on the back. "It looks like we are a team now, Randy. What do you think of that?"

It looked to me like Randy was tearing up. When he finally was able to speak, he said, "Matt, you are beyond generous. I think teaming up with Bill and the lab guys is a wise decision. If there really is Sasquatch holding that guy, you will need help. Besides, things have changed."

"What do you mean changed?"

"Well, it will be worth it even if you only get another two hundred coins. I am saying that because the twenty low-end $20 coins brought in more than I ever thought they would. Matt, I told you I thought those twenty coins might bring between $100,000 and $200,000. I was wrong, they brought $350,000."

"Wow! That's great, but why so high?"

"I was shocked, too. With the economy the way it is, gold has shot up. And these rare coins went up even higher. The big money collectors are looking for other places other than the stock market to put their money in, and they choose rare coins. So, you are in luck."

"No, Randy, *we* are in luck. If we recover Doug, there is a possibility to recover thousands of more coins as well. If that happens, everyone involved will benefit. The lab guys want to find and capture a Sasquatch. If they do, they will have what they want—recognition in their field. If we can bring back coins, everyone profits with wealth. And you and your collector friends profit from acquiring the greatest coins in existence. And if we free Doug, I profit from helping a person in need who has touched my life."

"It sounds like you have given this a lot of thought, Matt."

"I have, Randy. I have decided that I have been selfish, living alone, I've only thought of myself and my running. Running is satisfying, but I have spent too many years trying to achieve a goal that will never make me happy. Over the last week, I have become a part of something that makes a difference for many people, not just me. Doug has been held for six years and wants to be free. It was blind luck I found that pack. It will take teamwork to free him and I am tired of going solo. It feels great to be a part of this drive to help Doug. If we are successful in freeing him—and if we somehow bring a fortune back—I will be able to help many more people than just Doug."

Randy looked at me for a long time before he spoke. "Matt, you are quite a guy. You are being driven by a higher power than money. I'm glad you have decided to try rescuing Doug, and not just so we can get more coins. It's the right thing to do. And besides . . . just imagine if you really do find Sasquatch. That will really make the news and change your life. Once that happens, you might find it difficult to do your mountain training anymore."

"Why? I'm not going to let anything come between me and my training."

Randy started laughing hard, and it took a few minutes for him to be able to talk.

"What's so funny?"

"Oh, I was just imagining you racing for your life while being chased by a Sasquatch. Imagine how fast that would make your time!"

I had to laugh.

"So when are you leaving on this expedition?"

"That's what I started to tell you, Randy. I've got a time issue. We leave tomorrow morning."

"Tomorrow morning. That is quick."

"It is quick, but we have a limited timeline to find and free Doug this season. If we miss it, we will have to wait until next year for another chance. Which reminds me," I said as I pulled the bag of coins out of my backpack. "I am leaving all but ten of the lowest-value coins with you while I head out with the team. I am entrusting you to do your best to sell the coins."

I looked at Randy, who I had known for years and who had always been honest with me and said, "I'm trusting you here."

"Are you sure you want to leave them here?"

"Yes. You just confirmed your honesty by telling me you got $350,000 for the coins. You could have just as easily said you got $100,000."

"I've got to get going. We'll have to do that dinner we talked about next time. And go ahead and sell the coins you don't want to keep—the junk ones."

Randy laughed and said, "Not to worry, I'll do my best to raise the capital so you can save the world from the Sasquatch." He handed me a fat packet of money he had waiting in an envelope.

On the way out the door, I said, "I've kept ten coins just in case everything falls apart."

"That's good. With luck, there will be many more coins that can squirrel away for a rainy day if you find Doug."

I left Randy's shop, went straight to the bank to put the money in the safe deposit box, and then went home.

As I put the last few items in my packs and piled them by the door, I thought about what we'd be eating during our time in the wilderness. I sure hope Bill was bringing enough food. I knew Bill believed you can only think well on a proper diet, so he'd probably make sure everyone would have enough healthy and tasty food. Thinking about food made me aware that I'd better get a run in before dinner—a leisurely twelve-mile run, that is.

After my run, I stopped by Dick's Drive-In, my favorite hamburger place. It could be weeks before I'd get a chance to eat a hamburger again—if ever—I thought with a shiver. I'm a regular at Dick's, and my two deluxe burgers were as good as ever.

It was still early, so I drove around Green Lake on my way home.

The 2.86-mile trail was quiet tonight, with only a few joggers looping around the urban lake. I thought about all the hours I had trained there throughout my life and on the grass trails throughout the park surrounding Green Lake and the Woodland Park Zoo adjoining the park.

Back at home, I settled into bed, relaxed and confident. With what was ahead, I felt ready for battle, just like before a big race.

13

O n the way to the lab early Saturday morning, I was thinking about how my life had changed. A week ago, I was barely making my bills as a runner. Now I had gotten over $300,000 for only a small part of the coins I found. My life had been pleasant before, but a bit boring, until I found that backpack. A normal week for me would have been running six days a week, eating healthy, and sleeping too much. I rarely dated and didn't get out and meet many people besides other runners. Now I was heading out with a group of adventurous guys to search for a man held prisoner by Sasquatch. *My boredom has just packed up and left for good*, I thought.

I might have been the last to show, as the lab parking lot was buzzing with activity and high tension. Bill approached me as soon as I stepped out of my van.

"Looks like our Lou and Steve had a great night up on the trail," he said. "They took their bikes out on a few of the small game trails to the main Sasquatch trail and camped for the night. They've set up a base camp for themselves about thirty-seven miles from where we will have our base camp. Lou said the trail looks well-used and even groomed. It's not like any game trail they have ever seen, and quite different from the trails they rode in on. It looks like we may be on the right track about this being the Sasquatch trail. Not that I ever doubted you . . ."

"Not a problem," I said. "I still have a tough time believing all this is real."

Bill passed me the tablet he had been looking at. "This is going to be your main connection with me and everyone on this expedition if you are not wearing your headset. Once we are each set up with our personal mics and cameras, all information will be available. When you have your headset on, everyone can see and hear what you do. Like I said, watch what you look at or say."

It was amazing that I would be able to look at and zoom in on any pictures or videos that Steve and Lou take, as well as any video that came off anyone else's personal camera.

He instructed me to drive my van into the back of the lab so they could fit it with a powerful GPS and some computer gear that would help me track any of the trucks and the personal mic-camera setup we were all wearing.

Bill said, "It allows us to find any lost ducklings when we are out searching. Too bad our missing hiker, Doug, was not wearing the GPS tracker watch we are all wearing. We could have tracked him in real time using satellites. Even if you lose your mic and camera, we can still find you or anyone if they are wearing their GPS watch that I suggest everyone wear."

I wasn't sure if all this tracking stuff made me feel better or worse. I didn't want to think of what it would be like living with Sasquatch while waiting for someone to find me.

As the equipment installs were going on, one of the lab guys instructed me on how to use it. Fortunately, they installed a fancy voice-activated GPS and a ten-inch monitor. I would have a video screen to watch while I was in my van to see what was going on instead of using my heads-up display or tablet.

The expedition was finally ready to head out. Bill instructed everyone to turn on their monitors once they started their trucks, so we could all be synched together. "Don't want anyone to get lost," he added with a chuckle.

"Anyone could get lost in the woods without GPS," one of the guys hollered.

"True," Bill said, "but let's not get lost in downtown Seattle."

I was still smiling as I followed one of the guys and we all started off toward the mountains. Would we find Doug? Or maybe even a bit more treasure? I was excited to finally get started, but I knew the outcome was uncertain.

The trip from Seattle to Snoqualmie Pass only takes an hour on a good day, and the drive to the washed-out bridge was another forty-five minutes.

I parked my van by the river thirty feet from the washed-out bridge. I had given the guys lots of room to access the area around the bridge so they could set up all the equipment, including the portable trolley car, for crossing the river without getting soaked.

I could feel the excitement and anticipation as we made preparations to leave for the base camp. Bill only had to bark out one order and everyone knew exactly what they needed to do. I walked with Bill as he walked around to everyone in the group individually to ensure nothing was missing or needed.

He asked me, "Are you going to run up or ride the ATV?"

"I've been looking forward to riding the ATV if it's still OK." I had some comfort items with me and would need the ATV to haul them up.

Bill laughed and said, "Yeah, I'd sure rather ride the ATV than run uphill for miles myself."

Bill gave me a bit of instruction on an ATV, and I got my gear and strapped it on. A couple of the guys were setting up the equipment for the cable trolley using the bridge supports to anchor the cables. Everyone seemed to know what they were doing. Within an hour, the ATVs were loaded, and the cable trolley was operational. Some guys were even pulling trailers loaded with gear.

The last thing Bill handed out was the tranquilizer guns. Obviously, the men knew what to do with the guns because Bill just handed them out with extra ammo. When Bill got to me, he pulled me away from the group and showed me how to work the gun.

I felt comfortable with how to fire it but hoped I'd never have to. While Bill showed me how to work my gun, the guys moved the ATVs across the river using the cable trolley. Six ATVs were already across, and Bill motioned for me to drive my ATV onto the trolley next. Bill was the last across the trolley.

Once across the river, he said, "Go ahead, Matt, show us the way." It felt great leading the procession toward the cliff where I found the backpack. We left two guys back at the trucks to monitor communications and make sure we had everything covered.

Driving that ATV was fun. In fact, it was so fun I thought I'd get myself one to help move my gear for future distance runs. I was calm and relaxed until I got to the base of the cliff, where I found the backpack, and those weird feelings began again. At least this time, I had ten other guys with me to keep me company.

We started unloading the gear off the ATVs while some guys went up ahead to look for our best base camp site. Once the men above found the best spot, they threw a cable down from the top of the cliff. Two of the guys grabbed the cable and attached it to a tree forty feet from the cliff base. The men above hooked up a tripod and attached the assembly to a tree. Someone from above yelled down that the cable was set, Bill gave the orders to move all the equipment up to the new base camp using the new cable and a basket. I loaded my gear in the basket, and once it got pulled up, the men at the top took it and began setting up the base camp by the Sasquatch trail.

After watching the men assemble the river cable trolley and the cable basket set-up for their base camp, I grabbed a guy to help with my escape zip line before they took off to do their other assigned jobs.

"You afraid of sleeping on the ground?" one guy teased good-naturedly. They were probably all wondering why I'd need a half-mile zip line. He said, "Hey, that looks like a blast to play on." With a little help, I got my arboreal nest all put together, as well as the zip line, in less than thirty minutes. The lab guys had full climbing gear and went up the trees so fast I couldn't even get my climbing harness on before they dropped my rope ladder down and told me, "Tie this off, please."

Then one of the guys yelled, "Tie your gear to the next rope we drop, and we'll get you set up in a hurry." My tree perch was set about fifty feet off the ground in a bowl-like area of the tree. "You won't even need your tree hammock, this is so nice," one guy hollered.

"Not a chance, guys," I hollered back. "I plan on sleeping in comfort and safety."

When I got up there to inspect it, the guys had the hammock up and secured with all of my gear stowed inside. They had anchored the zip line about forty feet from my nest, making it easy to use but far enough away that others using it wouldn't disturb me, even if I was sleeping.

All I had to do if I wanted to use the zip line was walk forty feet across tree branches fifty feet off the ground holding on to a rope. I walked across to the zip line once to check it out and thought I might not want to play on it. Usually, when I sleep in a tree, it is only fifteen to twenty feet off the ground, just enough to keep out of reach of bears. Fifty feet off the ground is getting up there. I'd be keeping my harness on for sure and keep clipped onto a rope when walking around up there.

The guys said, "We had to set the zip line up that high to clear the ground and trees to make the full half-mile zip line work without hitting anything." They also were able to set the touch-down area next to a road that was a straight shot down to the trucks and Matt's van.

My tree hammock was as nice as any tent on the ground—and I even had my Lug-a-Loo porta-potty up there, so I wouldn't have to leave my tent in the middle of the night to go to the bathroom. Since I wouldn't have to cook either, I would be able to train and enjoy my time.

When I made it back to the ground, every bit of gear was put away and out of sight. Bill had picked this base camp spot because it was just 100 feet from the trail but completely hidden by rocks and trees. Even if we were out of sight, Bill had made sure everything was well hidden. It took me a while to make out the various camouflaged tents among the bushes and rocks. There were even camouflaged tree stands for men to sit in while on guard duty.

"How'd you guys hide all this equipment so fast?" I asked Bill.

"Oh, these guys have set up this kind of camp so many times, they could do it blindfolded or in the dark."

I followed Bill ten minutes walk down the trail to where two guys were working. He said, "This spot is a direct line of sight to our boy's camp about thirty-seven miles away. We decided to find a spot where we did not need to rely on electronics alone. Sometimes a good old-fashioned telescope can be your best bet for information, especially in a power outage situation. We'll monitor this telescope twenty-four hours a day as a backup system."

I was very impressed with how things were going and was beginning to have faith that they might be able to pull this rescue off.

I asked Bill, "When are we going to be wearing the headsets?"

"Why? Do you want to take a run and try one out?"

"That's exactly what I want to do. I want to see how I could use it in a race."

Bill looked at me, puzzled, so I explained. "Sometimes in a race, you want to see what is going on behind you, but it's not a good idea to turn and look, especially on rough courses, or you may go down. Also, I can ask for and get a map of where I am so I can take more routes without getting lost. It would also be fun to talk to someone on a long run or even ask a coach questions while training or racing."

"I get it, your coach or friends could watch the race from your perspective."

"Too cool if you ask me," I said.

"All right, Matt, in about fifteen minutes, we will have all the equipment linked and ready to fire up. By the time you climb back up to your nest and get your gear on, we will be ready to try out the system."

True to his word, Bill had the communication system running by the time I got back down from my nest. After some instructions, I felt ready to head out on a run.

Steve's was the first voice I heard over the com link after I turned it on. He was talking about the trail at their camp thirty-seven miles away. He was asking Bill if he and Stu could take the bikes further up the trail to explore. Bill was all for it but wanted everyone to be at their posts and up and running before Steve and Stu took off.

"Stay connected to the link twenty-four hours a day," Bill said to the whole group. There were a few chuckles before Bill added, "Yah, well, while you're sleeping or doing something personal, you can keep your mic off. But keep your earpiece in and working twenty-four-seven."

Lou chimed, "Well if you're doing hard labor or running, turn down the mic volume so everyone else does not have to listen to hard breathing." Then Lou added, "That goes for you, Matt, too. If you're going out for a two- or three-hour run, I don't want to listen to your deep breathing for that long."

I heard muffled laughter in the background and said, "I understand. But if I'm attacked by Sasquatch while running, and you don't hear it, it'll be your fault."

"Alright, guys," Bill announced, " time to clear the com link. Please get back to work, and earn your pay or treasure, whichever comes first."

There were whoops in the background, and the com went silent except for the occasional report.

I took the hint, turned my mic volume down on the comlink, waved goodbye over my shoulder, and started running down the Sasquatch trail toward Steve and Lou. There were thirty-seven miles to Steve and Lou's forward bike camp, and I didn't plan to run the whole distance.

The trail I was on was a good foot wider than a normal game trail, and two people could easily walk side by side on most of it. In many spots, it was even wider. The trail was as smooth as an old cinder running track and didn't have the sharp-edged rocks normally found on mountain trails. It was as if all the rocks had been walked on for so long that even they were now smooth.

This made running easier, and I was grateful as I would be able to run farther and much faster. The views from this ridge trail were fantastic. I could even see the spot on the trail thirty-seven miles away where Steve and Lou were camped, but I could not make out any details from this distance.

After about two and a half hours and almost twenty miles of running towards their camp, I still could not make out any details, but I could see the rockslide next to where they camped. I stopped, listened to the sounds of the forest, then turned around and headed back to camp. The trail was still as smooth twenty miles away from camp, and I wondered if this trail might be smooth for hundreds of miles.

Running back, I imagined setting up a race along this trail. From what Bill had found out about the trail using the satellite, the trail went the length of Washington State going north to south. The trail ended abruptly near every paved road or highway. It was obvious that whoever was using these trails did not want to be known. But how did they get from one section to the next? I knew Bill planned to find the answer of the trail's end on a future expedition.

Sporadic conversations came on over the comlink, but it was boring science talk, and I didn't pay attention for those last five hours running.

When I got back to camp, some of the lab guys came over to talk. They were eager for information about the trail or anything interesting I had seen. Bill and a couple guys who were runners came over to talk running.

"How can you run so far and fast and not even look tired?" one guy asked.

Bill wanted to check my vitals, and I agreed. He took my blood pressure, checked my heart rate, and did a few tests, then let out a whistle as he looked at me with a funny look on his face.

"What?"

"Have you had any lab tests done lately?" Bill asked.

"Not lately. Had physicals to run in high school and college, but I'm never sick and have never been in the hospital. Why do you want to know?"

"I want to know because you must have close to 100 percent slow twitch muscles, that is why."

I smiled and said, "Yeah, that's kind of what I think."

"It appears if your body is given enough food, it can sustain a nearly all-out effort without you getting tired."

I turned to Bill and said, "I know you are an ultra-runner who regularly races 100 to 250 miles and you have never lost a race. Is that correct?"

"Yes," Bill said, "that's true."

"What is your fastest mile time?"

"I haven't run one since college and it was slow. Now I only run a slower pace and do shorter runs," Bill said with a sigh.

I said, "My best mile time was a 4:16 during my junior year at college. After that, I only ran three-to-six-mile races but didn't do well until after college when I found I could run forever."

"Well," Bill said, "without doing a muscle biopsy, we can't know for sure, but your mile times during your races and workouts are always near your max pace, except when you are running a recovery pace. My guess is you are just a wonderful freak, just like our two tree-climbing freaks you've already met."

We sat down for a quick lunch, and afterward, I cleaned myself up in the solar shower, which even had warm water. That always felt wonderful after a long run. Bill didn't want us to use soap, deodorant, or any scented products while we were out here. We didn't want to leave a scent the Sasquatch could smell.

By then, I was ready for a nap, which is my normal routine. I put on my climbing harness and started up my fifty-foot rope ladder to my hammock. Sitting on a thick branch, I looked around. I could make out most of the camp through the branches, but I was well hidden. I could also see both ways quite a way down the trail, even as far as the spot with the telescope. Unzipping the hammock tent cover, I stepped inside, threw my sleeping bag over me, and turned my earpiece volume down low so I could sleep without interruption. I knew it would only take about thirty seconds for me to fall asleep after such a long run.

The call to dinner coming over my earpiece woke me.

The talk around dinner was about what they saw and the trail itself. No one had ever seen a game trail that looked so good. There were no areas damaged by washouts or slides, and it looked as if someone had repaired certain areas of the trail. The guys were also surprised at the absence of game animal tracks and droppings. It was as if animals stayed off the trail except to cross it. That was strange. What was it about the trail that kept indigenous animals off such a perfect trail? Our findings were identical to what Steve and Lou found thirty-seven miles away.

After Bill read the lookout schedule. I was surprised not to be on it and asked Bill about it.

"Well, Matt, this is all new to you. The rest of these guys have been here so often that they can react without hesitation and know the equipment. Besides, you need your sleep so you can do more long runs and entertain the rest of the team."

"What do you mean?" I asked.

The rest of the lab guys were smiling and nodding as Bill said, "As you know, Matt, most of the guys in this lab are active and an expedition such as this requires us to sit for most of the day.

Your five-hour run yesterday was just what this group needed. For years we have sat for days watching equipment doing our jobs happily but wanting to move. Whenever one of us needed a break earlier today while you were running, we would log in on your com-link video feed and enjoy the view.

"Think of your run as a travel video for scientists. We can enjoy the beautiful scenery you see as you run by or examine the terrain you have run past for further clues. I think I can speak for the guys . . . they just enjoyed watching while you ran. You did not say much while you ran, but your breath was a giveaway whenever you saw something beautiful. I could tell others were watching your run because sometimes there were sighs when you ran past a waterfall or steep cliff."

After dinner, some of us sat talking for a couple of hours until it started getting dark. Bill broke up the evening talk by reminding everyone they had work to do tomorrow and needed sleep to be 100 percent.

Before I went up to my perch Bill said, "Remember, climbing in the dark is much harder."

"Thanks, Bill," I said. After a few teasing remarks about the Boogeyman, everyone went off to settle into their own tents at ground level as I started the climb to my hammock. From my spot, I could see the crew's headlamps below in the gathering darkness. Looking up through the branches, I saw hundreds of stars. Tonight would be clear and a bit cold because we were at about 6,000 feet above sea level, but there was no rain or wind. Rain was not nearly as bad as the wind, especially fifty feet above the ground. Lying up there, I thought about how trees can sway enough to throw you off your branch to the ground, which is why I always wore my climbing harness, even in my sleeping bag. I had anchored my safety rope to the tree before going into my hammock tent.

As usual, I slept well and woke up at 5:00 a.m. as usual. By 6:00 that Sunday morning, everyone was up and at their stations. Bill went over the day's schedule while we ate breakfast. My day was totally open, so I offered to deliver coffee and anything anyone wanted or needed. While I was walking around doing that, a call came in that had the whole team buzzing around like angry bees.

14

"There's something coming!" Steve's voice had come over the com at 8:05 that morning. Steve and Lou, the crazy mountain bikers and forward lookouts, had been in place for almost forty-eight hours and had been considering calling Bill to see if they could take off on some fun riding when they spotted a procession coming their way.

He said, "It looks like some humans and some larger hairy humanoids with them."

Lou broke in and said, "They look like they're about fifteen miles from us, moving at a steady walking pace. At that rate, they'll take about five hours to reach us."

Steve said, "We really want to ride out a bit to get closer. What do you think?"

"Go ahead," Bill said, "but keep at least a mile of separation so you can easily get away if you need to."

At first, we could hear them excitedly singing, "Yipee ti yi yo, get along, little doggies," and then saying something about lassoing a Sasquatch.

Bill reminded them, "Remember my rule is 'Don't take chances.'" He talked to them about using distance and being cautious and told them to keep their helmet mikes on so the whole team could keep track.

I thought that was another way of Bill saying, "Shut up and get to work."

Steve and Lou took off slowly and easily, so they wouldn't raise dust even though the procession was so far away. As they rode along the mountain ridge, they caught a glimpse of the procession off in the distance when they pulled over and used their satellite-guided telescope.

After about twenty minutes, Bill told Steve and Lou to pull over. Both men followed protocols, pointed their bikes back towards camp, set all bike systems on pause for a quick start up, and then took off on foot. He reminded them to always stay close to their bikes and keep at least one mile between themselves and the procession.

Steve and Lou walked over to the edge of the ridge, keeping a large boulder between themselves and the procession. Once in place, they set up the telescope and, in moments, located the procession still coming their way.

Steve softly spoke into his mic, saying, "We're locked onto the procession and have a clear picture. There are two humans and nine hairy humanoids."

The whole camp and the boys at the trucks all started talking at once. It took Bill quite a while to settle the group down and get them working on monitoring the sound and video Steve and Lou were broadcasting. Once the men saw the first video frames, they dove into their work like real scientists and began the job of trying to determine what these beings were. Everyone read their monitoring equipment, and in turn, each person called out any information they had gathered. Someone called out the height, others called out weight, gender, body temperature of each subject, and what they suspected the species to be—Sasquatch, hybrid, or human.

After twenty minutes, Steve said, "They're within 2.2 miles of our position." Next, he called in to say, "We're gonna move. They're now within 1.25 miles . . . unless you want us to stay longer and keep the video rolling?"

"Grab the equipment and hotfoot it to the bikes and drop back to your original position eight miles back," Bill said.

"Moving already," Steve said.

Bill called out to everyone and asked, "Have you got enough information? Or would you like Steve and Lou to set up their equipment once they're back in position?"

"We're good on info," someone said. "But if possible, we'd like to watch if Steve and Lou can set up again."

I was thinking the same. We all wanted to just watch the Sasquatch walk.

"We'd all like to watch. But just keep it safe—and keep radio silence," cautioned Bill.

Every one of us had our headset coms on, even the guys at the trucks, so we all heard the "rum, rum" of the bikes coming to life and starting down the trail.

Just then, we heard Lou's voice in a hushed whisper, "What the ? . . . My bike just quit."

"What happened? Bill asked.

"I don't know! My bike just quit. All the lights are off."

Then Steve's voice came on. "Mine's not working either."

Bill looked like he was about to come unglued. "Can you coast?"

Steve shot back, "We've got about a half a mile hill downhill but then a steep climb from there."

"Coast as far and as fast as you can, then grab your gear and get out of there!"

Bill did not have to tell them twice. Steve and Lou tucked and coasted down that hill as fast as they could. Then they got off their bikes, ran them as far away from the trail as possible, and quickly ditched them.

Neither man spoke as they quickly gathered all the gear they thought they would need, including the tranquilizer guns, and started a slow run back to camp.

We could see the path they were taking through our headsets. They were moving fast, as if they were anxious to get more distance between them, although the procession was still a mile away. Both guys were in decent shape, and I thought they were easily capable of running the eight miles back to their base camp at more than twice the speed of the procession.

Then we saw Steve and Lou had made it back to their base camp. It had taken them just over an hour to go the eight miles back to their camp. They were now forty-five miles away but could probably make it to us in eight to ten hours if they left some of their equipment, food, and tents behind.

They would know they could not keep a fast pace for another thirty-seven miles. We could see Steve setting up the telescope so they could see how much more ground they had put between themselves and the Sasquatch procession. Lou was gathering the hydration packs and food rations and energy bars for their trip back. He grabbed the water bottles, two running hip packs that could carry four one-liter bottles and a water filtration pump and slipped it into the hip pack. While Lou was loading energy bars into each pack, Steve was trying to find the procession.

Bill was talking to Steve, trying to help with the electronic telescope. For some odd reason, it wasn't firing up. It was strange—it had quit just like the electric bikes had.

"Reboot it and see if that helps," Bill told him in his ear.

Right when I was thinking, *Just get out of there! Don't bother taking pictures and just go!* we heard Steve say, "We're gonna take off. Just carrying the essentials—and for sure the tranquilizer guns."

"Just get back here as fast as you can," Bill said. "Leave all equipment you don't need to make it back to camp safely."

Steve's answer stopped in mid-word and we heard him holler something that sounded like ". . . big ass, hairy . . ." I knew it was him because he had a distinctive voice. A tree branch had hit him in the throat while he was riding his mountain bike down a steep trail three years earlier. After ten days in the hospital, his voice sounded like Donald Duck on nitrous oxide.

Then his mic went silent. Lou's mic went dead at the same time, though we hadn't heard him say a word.

Terry, one of the techs, said, "Maybe something blocked the mic and video signal. There's no way both personal systems could go out at the same time without affecting our comlinks." Terry explained Steve and Lou were getting their com signal via satellite. All the comlink signals were being sent by satellite, so if it was the comlink, then everyone's comlink in the party should also have gone out. He said, "If we have signals and Steve and Lou don't, then something near them is blocking the signal."

"What could have done it?" Bill asked.

"I don't understand it," Terry said. "Even I wouldn't be able to knock out two high-tech headsets without blocking the signals from all the rest. We're all connected. Whatever happened was something that shouldn't be able to happen. And it's happening right near Lou and Steve."

Bill asked, "Who's monitoring the headset cameras?"

Gus spoke up, "I am. And I'm already going over the videos from Steve and Lou's headset cameras." Gus and Joe were at the trucks for an emergency backup.

"Let me know as soon as you find something."

After hearing Steve shout out, my stomach was clenching, and I kept looking around. We thought we were prepared for any eventuality. But we were hunting intelligent creatures. And now, something had gone very wrong.

Bill said, "Look for anything that would explain the blocked signal. We need to see what's going on. Anything you produce is better than what we have now, so start thinking like the smart scientists you are."

Gus called in again and said, "I've got something! Click on Steve's icon and look at the video from his feed from twelve seconds before it died."

There were gasps as we all saw the same video display. At twelve seconds before Steve and Lou's mics went dead, Steve's camera caught a few seconds of something sneaking into the frame. Steve was looking down at the electronic telescope while he was talking to Bill and must not have seen what his camera picked up.

We were all looking at a large, very hairy arm reaching for Steve, and then the camera went dark.

Terry said, "The Sasquatch must have done something to Steve and Lou's personal comlinks. Look at the video closely . . . the com goes offline before the Sasquatch touches Steve. Its hand was still six or more inches away from Steve when the com died. Somehow it shut the comlink down!"

One of the other guys said, "Are you saying these creatures possess advanced electronic capabilities?" Then everyone talked at once and I couldn't make out a word. All of us were replaying those last twelve seconds of Steve's comlink, trying to figure out what happened.

Then Gus spoke up again. "It might be my larger screens in the truck down here, but I may have solved a part of the mystery."

"What did you find?" asked Bill, the tension in his voice obvious.

"I can see the video better on my bigger screen. When I look closely at a small area on the wrist of the Sasquatch under magnification, I see something that looks like gray metal on the hairy wrist of the hand reaching for Steve. It appears to be electronic and the size of a cell phone. If these Sasquatch can knock out the coms the way they did, they have more advanced technology than we do."

Bill asked, "Are you thinking that bit of technology on its wrist can possibly do more than knock out our little satellite com?"

Our thoughts were going wild. Could it be that the Sasquatch had developed an advanced civilization that went far beyond their trail building? Had they advanced much farther than that by many times over? We had seen no signs of technology or manufacturing out here in the northern forests of Washington. How could they possibly be developing technology?

Then Joe spoke up from down at the trucks. "If these Sasquatch are real, then their civilization may be ancient. They could have been here for millions of years. Their society may be hidden. Just because we can't see it doesn't mean it doesn't exist."

Then I couldn't help it, I had to speak up. "Don't you remember the hidden caves and rooms the diary talks about? If they have electronics, why can't they have underground manufacturing and living quarters?"

Bill said, "We'd be making a mistake to underestimate these creatures."

"Yeah, we could be in trouble ourselves," one of the techs said.

"Does anyone want to leave right now and head back to the truck?" Bill asked. He waited for a few seconds in silence before he went on. "I am not asking anyone to risk their lives here. I am asking for ideas on how we can protect ourselves if we stay. In light of the coms going down, I don't know if it's possible to capture a Sasquatch. We now know our links will probably go down if they approach or attack. We need a different plan than we currently have if we are going to stay."

I couldn't help speaking up. "All this talk of tech and coms! We have to get Steve and Lou back—that's the main thing, not the tech or snatching a Sasquatch so we'll be famous or finding more gold so we'll be rich!"

"You're right. Think of Steve and Lou. Let's make a plan," said Bill.

I was on a roll and said, "How about we ambush the Sasquatch from the trees when they come?" After I said that, I wished I hadn't because it sounded so simple and stupid. So very low-tech. The silence told me the others were probably being kind right now because Steve and Lou had been taken, so they weren't going to tease me for such a bad idea.

"Well," Gus spoke up, "that's not a bad idea. If most men are in the trees, and a couple of men are on the ground as bait, it could work. Remember, the diary said the Sasquatch can't climb, so the guys in the trees should be safe and able to shoot the Sasquatch with the tranquilizer guns and protect the guys on the ground."

Bill took a vote and everyone agreed to stay. The plan seemed solid. Joe and Gus would drive the remaining ATVs up to their location loaded with the extra tranquilizer guns and tranquilizer darts as well as any tree climbing equipment they could load on and still make it up the hill to them.

With Gus and Joe joining them, there would be six men in the trees shooting, not just four. It might not be enough to have two men on the ground if things got hot in a fight. We would draw straws for who would remain on the ground.

We figured it would take at least twenty-four hours before the Sasquatch would arrive and twice that if they kept the pace they were going in, the videos we had seen before Steve and Lou were taken.

It was now about 5:30 p.m., and the light was dimming. It was too late for Gus and Joe to gather the gear, load the ATV and get here without having to use headlights. We couldn't risk the Sasquatch catching sight of their headlights. Gus and Joe would load the ATV tonight, move it across to the other side of the river with the trolley, and leave at first light. They should arrive with the extra guns, ammo, and tree gear by 7:00 a.m. Plenty of time for the guys who were setting up in the trees to get into a secured position for the encounter with the Sasquatch later that day or the next.

"Look for a tree or cliff face that will allow you to sleep and still have a good line of sight to shoot your guns," said Bill, who was clearly rattled. "And take some food and water with you. We don't know how long we'll be in the trees."

As the guys were choosing their spots, I thought about the two unlucky guys who were going to be bait. I wouldn't want to be sleeping on the ground right below the tree stands when the Sasquatch came along.

Within a couple of hours, the men found over a dozen spots and set about turning them into sleeping spots and sniper nests.

Bill walked over to me and said, "I don't want you involved in the shooting. My men and I have worked together for over seven years and are all proficient with our weapons. No offense, but if it comes to a battle, you might mess us up. It would be better for all of us if you just hung back."

"I want to help, but I hear you," I told Bill. "I've never even fired a gun before."

"OK, Matt, your job will be to monitor the attack if one happens and keep everyone informed on what you see."

I thought about Bill's comments as I began the fifty-foot climb to my nest. I had picked this tree in the first place because it was tall and easy to climb, and it was on the cliff facing the trucks seven miles away by the road. I had a crazy idea about using my zip line to get as far away from camp as possible, then run back to the top to sneak in a workout. If I needed to escape, the zip line would be my way to get away fast.

I looked around me at the trees the other men had chosen for their tree stands. They were all lower than mine. When they first started talking about tree nests, I had told everyone they needed to be as high as they could go.

"The diary said the Sasquatch don't climb, so we don't need to be that high," one of the guys said. "If we are any higher, we won't be able to hit the Sasquatch with the tranquilizer dart guns."

I looked down from my perch and saw most of their tree stands were twelve to fifteen feet off the ground.

I had told them, "A seven-foot-tall basketball player could jump that high," but nobody seemed to be paying attention to what I was saying.

"We'll be able to shoot the Sasquatch before it can jump that high."

Chatter and noise came from the tree nests and from the ground. Everyone seemed excited about an encounter that might happen by tomorrow afternoon. Because of the pace they were going, no one seemed worried about the Sasquatch getting there early. I wasn't surprised that night when most of them didn't sleep in their new nests but stayed on the ground instead.

Me? You couldn't have paid me any amount of money to get me to sleep on the ground that night. But the other guys opted to spend one more night on a comfortable sleeping pad on firm ground instead of sleeping in the trees since the Sasquatch would not be there for a day or two.

Bill held one last meeting before bedtime. He told us they had not gotten visual contact by satellite or any electronic methods since Steve and Lou's coms went down. Using the telescope, we had a visual of the procession leaving Steve and Lou's base camp about thirty minutes after their coms went down. But because they kept just inside the trees most of the time, we were unable to ascertain who or how many were in the group. After they rounded a bend, they had not been seen since. Bill floated the possibility that they had left the trail and gone in a different direction, but we were proceeding with our plans as if they would arrive sometime after noon the next day.

He assigned positions along the trail in case of an encounter. All the hidden ambush positions had been adjusted so they were all in a line of sight to one another. This would allow us to communicate verbally in case we lost electronics.

When he was done, the light was beginning to fade, and Bill announced, "Lights out. I really mean no lights tonight, guys. All electronics except com links need to be put into sleep mode so we do not have any lights showing. Gentlemen, see you in the morning." Then Bill walked over to his tent . . . on the ground.

I climbed my ladder listening to the settling down noises below me. Each night I had spent in my hammock, I had pulled up the ladder. That night was exceptionally quiet and I felt safe lying in my sleeping bag high above the ground. It was as though no birds, animals, or insects were out tonight, although there was a full moon. With the tension in the air, I knew sleep would be hard, so I lay back, cleared my mind, and practiced my relaxing techniques until I finally fell asleep.

15

_____

I awoke to scuffling sounds below. Quickly glancing at my watch in the moonlight, I saw it was 2 a.m. I was about to holler down to whoever was making all the noise when I heard sounds I could not identify. Between sounds of scuffling, moans, and yelling, I heard a language I couldn't make out and it didn't sound human. We had been found by the Sasquatch!

How did they get here so quickly?

The sounds intensified as all hell had broken out below. I could hear equipment being thrown around and the loud pops of the tranquilizer guns being fired.

"The tranqs aren't working," a guy shouted.

That wasn't sounding good. Our main defense was down.

"My coms are out," yelled another.

I checked my communication line and found mine was still working. The realization that I could be the only one at base camp with a working com line hit me.

"Come in, base camp," I heard Gus down at the trucks yell in my ear. "Do you copy?" But I was too afraid to say a thing, or be heard, so I turned my mic off, and turned the volume down, but kept listening to the voices of Gus and Joe.

"Shoot 'em," came the shout from below. Then, one by one, the men's voices below me were silenced. Some voices stopped in mid-word and others with a scream.

The fight below lasted less than three minutes before it was completely silent again on the ground.

Now I could only hear Gus and Joe talking about making the drive to base camp as soon as it was light enough to start.

"We'll take the tranquilizer guns off the ATV and most of the other gear," Joe said. With the extra gear off, we'll be faster and more maneuverable."

"We'll show up with the big guns and kick some furry butt!" said Gus. After that show of bravado, he sounded more subdued, "We should try and sleep for the next few hours if we can."

I kept very still. I could hear the sounds of someone or something walking below. I could hear the sounds of equipment being gathered and stacked near the trail. All the while, the Sasquatch talked among themselves in their weird unintelligible language.

Then I heard something that caused a trickle of tension at the back of my neck. *Was that an English word I heard?* Maybe one of our guys was alright. There it came again. No, it was someone swearing in English. Do the Sasquatch speak our language?

Afraid that the creatures below would hear me breathe or maybe even smell me, I lay motionless in my sleeping bag, fifty feet above them. Around 5:30, the early light allowed me to make out shapes. I didn't want to see the creatures below, but I needed to know what was going on if I was going to survive this.

I rolled onto my side until I could see over the edge of the hammock to the ground below. There were two humans—two men—standing together. I could tell they were not from the lab by their clothing, so they must be traveling with the Sasquatch. One was short for a human, and one was tall. Were these the captives Doug and Mike from the diary?

Should I try to get their attention? No, too risky. I didn't know whose side they were on.

Right then, the guy I thought must be Doug spoke in English.

"The Sasquatch think there is one more human here. There is a human odor still close. Our friends sure do have good noses," said the short one.

The bigger guy said, "I overheard one of the leaders say they will wait until daylight and do a full visual and equipment scan for the missing human. Looks like we have a few hours of work ahead of us, Mike."

Now I knew Doug was the tall one and Mike was the short guy with him. *Can I trust them*? Not sure, I just kept quiet and watched.

Then in my ear, I heard Gus say, "There's something wrong with the ATV. It just will not start."

"Crap," said Joe, "now we'll have to walk."

Gus and Joe spent the next few minutes making plans. They knew it was about seven miles, mostly uphill. Joe said, "That should take us a little over three hours carrying as many guns and as much ammo as we can. If we push it hard, we can get up to the camp around 8:30. But we'll have to leave soon."

"We don't even know what's going on up there. Maybe there's just a major breakdown of the coms preventing them from contacting us," said Gus.

"Or maybe the Sasquatch showed up early and are not peaceful . . ." said Joe. "But we've got to try to at least help our team. If we encounter the Sasquatch, do you think we should try to negotiate with them?"

"Huh," grunted Gus. "They'll take one look at our guns, and that'll do the negotiating."

* * *

By 7:00 a.m., the sun was up, and I could see everything clearly down below. I knew Gus and Joe were probably on the way by now. The Sasquatch and the two humans were over by the pile of gear and ATVs about 100 feet away. That gave me some breathing room.

I had slept in my clothes, as I was nervous about what might happen and wanted to be ready, so I eased carefully out of my sleeping bag. Quickly grabbing some food packs and water, I stuffed them in my running pack.

It was seven miles downhill to my van, but as I had seen the last two days, anything could go wrong. I had to get to Joe and Gus before they got too far from the trucks and got captured like the others. *If I can get going soon, I can intercept them before they get halfway up the trail. Then we can run back to the trucks ahead of the Sasquatch.*

I put my feet into my lightest racing shoes because I'd need speed for this trail run. All the while, I was careful not to shake the branches with my movements. I didn't know if I could run faster than a Sasquatch, but I was sure I had more endurance.

Bill had estimated the Sasquatch weighed over seven hundred pounds each. There was no way anything that big could run far, even if they were fast. If a Sasquatch tried to run fast for too long, it would quickly overheat, like a bear. I knew bears could run fast, but not for long before they had to cool down in water or by digging into the cool dirt and lying down.

I figured if I could get a big enough lead, I should be able to wear the Sasquatch down in a quarter mile or a half mile at most.

I know! I'll use the zip line! That would give me at least a half-mile lead by the time I hit the ground. I knew I'd have to "hit the ground running," as the proverbial phrase goes, or they would grab me.

Wearing only a tank top, light racing shorts, socks, ultra-light trail racing shoes, a GPS watch, my headset, and my running hip pack, I got ready to make my move. There would be enough water on the trail, so I could save weight by not carrying a lot of heavy water. I quietly raised my water bottle to my lips and drank so I'd be hydrated enough to run the seven or more miles without needing to drink. I didn't usually drink during a 10K (6.2 miles), so it wouldn't be a big deal anyway.

I knew it was up to me to get out safely, so I could organize a rescue for Bill and the other nine guys. The few guys back at the lab knew where we were and where to start looking, but they would need me to tell them what happened.

If I didn't make it back, at least Randy had the coins he could keep or sell. I didn't want to think about not making it back. All those dreams about being rich after locating the Sasquatch gold didn't mean as much to me right then.

I did have something I needed to do urgently and as quietly as possible. Finally, the Lug-a-Loo turned out to be essential. Never mind all those guys who had teased me about it.

My watch said it was chilly, forty-two degrees. I grabbed a small polar fleece blanket to throw over my shoulders, planning to ditch it once I started running. With one last look over the edge, I carefully climbed out of my hammock nest and onto the tree branch. Tensing my muscles, I painstakingly started for the zip line forty feet away from my perch.

When I put the zip line in, I placed it in a good spot to get downhill fast, not for its convenience from my hammock. Now I had to climb forty feet across tree branches fifty feet off the ground. The thought of doing that with 700-pound hairy beasts below that wanted to capture me and were searching for me made me start to sweat.

It took me five minutes to go the first thirty feet, moving quietly and slowly. I was grateful there was a breeze blowing, so the branches were naturally moving. At times I had to crawl across larger branches with open space between the branches because of the danger of being seen. Then just as I was about to step across a wide-open area with two Sasquatch walking right below, a gust of wind hit me and my blanket blew off my shoulders and began falling towards the ground.

I didn't stop to think, I just dove for the falling blanket. Somehow, I hooked my feet under a large branch as I fell forward and grabbed a branch with my left arm. If I had fallen, it would have meant fifty feet to my death, but if the blanket had fallen, I would have been discovered.

For now, I was alive and unhurt. I didn't hear shouting below, so the wind must have masked the sounds of me falling onto another branch. I was holding myself up by my ankles and my left arm. My right arm was hanging down in space and felt numb as my right hand had caught the blanket that I was clutching so tightly my hand was white.

When I dared to look below, I saw the ground with nothing for me to grab if I fell. Two Sasquatch were walking away to my left as if nothing had happened.

I lifted my arm, clutching the blanket over my head and tucked it into the tree branches around the opening I had almost dived through. With my right hand now free, I pulled myself back up onto the branches. I grabbed the blanket, though, for a moment, I thought about leaving it behind. But if it took me into the night to get out of here, I'd need it to keep warm. Tying the blanket around my waist, I walked the last ten feet to the zip line.

Relief flooded through me as I reached it. *I might have a chance now.* The zip line would give me a big head start. Once I got on the ground, I was confident I could run to my van. *It's funny,* I thought, *I'd be running the most important race of my life and there was no one to watch.*

Then my eyes shot wide open as I remembered the com gear I was wearing. *Oh, heck, Gus and Joe can watch!* I activated the com unit's full functions and flipped out the heads-up display screen. The technician said it could record both forward and backward videos at the same time. I had thought at the time it would be a great way to film a race. Now it would be put to good use. The video would be sent to the trucks, the lab, and my display, so it couldn't be lost. There would be a record. Someone would know what happened to me.

If I did escape and get back, at least I would have proof and would be able to get help to save the other guys. With the flip-out heads-up screen, I could see through the screen to run but also see who was behind me. I couldn't help but imagine what this film showing me running away from—and hopefully escaping—from the Sasquatch would be worth to the media.

Before I got on the zip line, I had turned the earpiece sound off on the com unit so the Sasquatch or humans couldn't hear it, but now I turned it back on, careful to leave the mic off. I wanted to know how Gus and Joe were doing before I made my escape.

Between the heavy intakes of breath coming into my ears, I heard Gus say, "Looks like we'll get to the camp about 8:30."

Joe said, "Man, this gun is getting heavy. I don't want to be too tired to fight if we need to."

"Well, we could cut the pace a little." More heavy breathing.

I knew I'd have to leave very soon to have a hope of reaching them before the halfway point. It would only take me fifteen or twenty minutes to reach them and then another twenty minutes going a race pace to reach the trucks. I'd have to figure out then whether to run ahead or stay with the guys, as I knew they couldn't keep up with me.

Just before I was ready to push off, I thought about the noise the zip line was going to make. How could I make it quieter? No idea. I was about to give up and just jump on, ride it as far and fast as it could go and take my chances when I thought about the blanket. Could I make it work like a muffler to smother the noise?

I wrapped the blanket around the cable carefully and thought about using the bottoms of my shoes as brakes so I wouldn't go too fast and make too much noise. *Maybe they won't even hear me*, I thought.

Once I hit the road, I figured I'd have over a mile of lead over the Sasquatch. Even if they could run thirty miles an hour, it would take them at least a mile to catch me. From what Doug said in the diary, I didn't believe the Sasquatch would be able to run after a mile—and they would still have to run two miles before they would catch me.

Harness on, I gave a quick snap, kicked my legs and grabbed the cable with my feet. I placed the arch of each shoe around the cable and squeezed as my shoes touched and started rolling to test my brakes. As soon as my shoes touched the cable, I stopped rolling. My brakes worked! I began rolling slowly, and hopefully quietly, down the cable to safety.

About twenty feet down the zip line, still a good fifty feet before I'd go over the edge and shoot down a steep incline for almost half a mile. The wheels of the zip line pulleys barely made any noise, and I didn't think those fifty feet away could hear it. About twenty feet from the main downhill, I felt I was almost free and allowed myself to relax just a bit.

Just as I slowed down my speed before the steep incline part of the zip line, I heard a noise below me. Putting more pressure against the cable with my shoes, I slowed to a stop, thinking it would be better to stay hidden if possible. Gus and Joe were still far enough away that the Sasquatch would not reach them, so taking a bit more time to keep hidden was probably a good idea.

Below me, I could see some Sasquatch were still searching the area. They sniffed the air but never looked up.

I froze and tried not to even breathe until the Sasquatch walked at least forty feet away. Waiting another minute, I loosened the grip of my feet and began moving again. After I went around the corner, the angle quickly became steep. I had to tighten my grip to the max to avoid rolling out of control. The zip line was meant to go fast, and it took all my strength to keep the speed low.

Swiveling my head, I saw I had dropped about 150 feet below the cliff top, so I let loose with my feet and began picking up speed. I was tearing down the hill at nearly full speed when suddenly, the pulley above my head started screeching loudly and the whole thing came to a stop. Going forward at top speed, my harness line stopped me dead, and I had the wind knocked out of me.

After I could finally breathe again, it was still a good fifteen seconds before my head started to clear. I felt cold, and my chest and legs were constricted by the harness straps. *What happened?* One look told me it was that darn blanket again. At the highest speed, the blanket had flown up and caught in the pulley. Earlier, it had been keeping things quiet, but now it was making the pullies scream. I silently cursed that blanket and wished I had worn long pants and a long top so I wouldn't have grabbed the blanket in the first place.

Oh no, the Sasquatch must have heard the screech for sure! They would be trying to locate the source of that sound.

I looked at my watch and could not believe my eyes. It had been 7:27 when I left the corner after seeing the Sasquatch and it was now 7:28. I had only lost about thirty seconds or so. If I acted fast, I could still get away before the Sasquatch figured out what was making that sound and found me. With luck, I could free myself and be at the bottom in less than a minute.

I hoped.

If I had at least a minute before they arrived, it would give me enough time to get away. That is if the lab guys had correctly figured out the Sasquatch endurance profiles.

Big if.

I had to try, so I pulled myself up and began tugging on the pulley to free the blanket. I thought about pulling myself back uphill and rolling out of the tangle, but the pulleys didn't budge. Less than a minute later, while I was still trying to untangle the blanket, I heard excited Sasquatch-speak coming from the cliff top above, the one I had just left.

One look was all I needed. I swung my legs up, hooked them around the cable, and tried to free the blanket with all my might. I had left my knife behind to keep the weight down, and now I cursed that decision.

By this time, it had been over two minutes since I heard the Sasquatch above me, and I had not freed even one inch of the blanket. Now I could hear Sasquatch below me and downhill further along the path of the zip line.

I'm going to get caught, I thought. Feelings of despair rushed through me. I imagined being captured and held prisoner for over a hundred years until even the last person I knew on earth was long gone, and I was still alive and held prisoner.

I counted at least eight Sasquatch above, below, and down along the zip line. It was just a matter of time before they had me. And I was stuck at least seventy feet above rocks on a very steep cliff face.

Then I had an idea. I knew it was a long shot, but it might work. If I could wrap my legs tightly around the cable so I could slip out of the harness, I could unhook the safety harness from the pulley system, hang on with my legs, and I'd be free to go down the zip line cable without using the stuck pulley system.

I didn't think about it for another second. I unbuckled my harness and freed myself as the Sasquatch-talk got louder and sounded more excited. I had to slip one leg at a time off the cable to slip out the leg loops. Right then, I was grateful that I was thin and flexible, or I wouldn't have been able to hold on. I probably looked like a contortionist doing a high-wire act for the Sasquatch below and above as I unhooked my chest strap and let the safety line slip off each shoulder. That safety line was all that kept me from falling. Now I'd have to depend upon myself alone.

For a split second, I went into myself, just as I do before every race. I asked myself, *Why are you doing battle?*

To my surprise, the answer that popped into my head was, *It's better than being normal.* I knew I had changed since I found the diary. I was a part of this crazy expedition to rescue Doug with Bill and the other lab guys. We had become instant friends. Deciding to mount the rescue in the first place helped me grow as a person. I was taking responsibility like a man.

I was doing battle to save others. I had to outrun the Sasquatch so I could come back for Bill and the guys and Doug and the others. But I had to act quickly before Gus and Joe got too close for a comfortable escape. *I'm doing battle to live to fight another day,* I said to myself. If I get out of here, we'd have to mount a rescue with many more people next time.

If I get out of here . . .

These thoughts passed through my mind in seconds. The Sasquatch were still making a lot of noise by the time I opened my eyes and looked around.

I heard something above and looked up at a sight I never expected to see. A human I had never seen before was doing something at the corner of the zip line at the top of the cliff. It looked like he was trying to attach something to slide down to me.

I wasn't waiting around to find out what he was doing. I had a bright idea. I could use my hip-pack. Made of Kevlar, it was light, bulletproof, and friction- and heat-resistant. If I could unbuckle the pack, slip it over the cable, and grab an end with each hand, then I could use it to slide down the cable. But this all had to be done while hanging from a cable seventy feet above rocks by just using my legs! I could not take a chance of dropping the pack, so I hung on tightly with my legs and my head hanging down.

The Sasquatch saw what I was doing and got really excited. They pointed up at me and were yelling something to the human up above by the corner. Maybe they thought I was going to let go and fall and were telling the human to get to me quickly. I wasn't waiting around and reached for my hip pack with both hands and undid the buckle.

I felt the weight of the pack as it came free from my waist and thought, *How is something this light going to protect me*? I pulled myself up and looped the pack over the cable. When I went to swing the pack over the cable, I knew I was going to have to let go of the pack with both hands. That scared me a whole lot, but it went over without a hitch. Now I held one strap in each hand.

After adjusting the main part of the hip pack so the thickest part was in the middle riding over the cable, I looped the waist strap around each hand and made sure it was snug. After one last look back to the corner, I saw the human was almost ready to leave, so I said a prayer, dropped my legs down from the cable and started sliding. Quickly picking up speed, I was flying like the cable was greased because the Kevlar on the pack was tough and as smooth as silk.

But what would happen at the end in less than a half mile—less than one minute away? I did not have a brake to stop myself! How would I stop?

I looked ahead and saw something that nearly broke me. The Sasquatch had reached the bottom of the zip line. Two were waiting for me at the bottom by a tree—the very tree I would crash into unless something slowed me down.

Then I thought of how, as a kid, my brothers and I would "parachute." We'd climb trees, jump onto smaller thin trees from above, and ride them to the ground. If I could drop at the right time, I could do the same thing. The only thing that gave me pause was I'd be doing it at close to thirty miles per hour.

I would aim for a tree below the tree I was heading for. The trees below were close to one another and small enough so they should bend easily, even at my weight. Hopefully, I wouldn't get hurt—much.

Taking a deep breath, I let go. The drop to the treetops was only about twenty feet, but I was still fifty feet off the ground when I started falling. My forward speed was still fast, so I whipped through the first few trees until my speed slowed enough, and crashed lower down into a slightly thicker tree and completely stopped. Then I began falling through the thinner top branches.

Finally, I stopped about fifteen feet from the ground. Shaken and bruised, I ignored the pain signals in my body. My desire to avoid being caught by the Sasquatch overrode my pain as I began climbing down as fast as I could. The last branch was only about ten feet from the soft dirt and moss below, so I dropped to the ground and started running.

There was no thought in my mind about starting slow. I was running almost flat out once I started. Behind me, I heard lots of excited yelling, mostly in the weird Sasquatch language. As I rounded the first corner on the dirt road, the sounds of human voices mixed with the unintelligible sounds behind.

Mike and Doug must also be with the Sasquatch! I wasn't concerned about the humans catching up to me, as I ran at a world-class speed. The sounds of my chase group faded as I opened the distance from them. I figured I would outrun the Sasquatch after the first mile and wasn't too worried about Mike and Doug.

Gus and Joe should still be halfway down the road from the trucks. Hopefully, I could reach them with a big enough lead so we'd all make it back to the river safely. Ahead there was a straightaway almost half a mile long, so I'd soon be able to tell what sort of lead I had.

But less than halfway down the straightaway, I heard the sounds of runners behind me and turned for a quick look. I couldn't believe it, but the Sasquatch were running as expected, but Mike and Doug were running with them—and they were gaining! There was no way humanly possible that those two should be able to run that fast. I was one of the fastest humans on earth and these two were gaining on me.

Mike was short and heavy, so it should be impossible for him to run that fast. Doug was tall but not a trained runner, so he also should not be that fast. Yet they were both gaining.

As I ran into the next corner onto another straightaway, I saw Gus and Joe sprinting uphill toward me.

"Turn around and run!" I yelled at them, not stopping.

It took Gus and Joe a couple of seconds to understand there was danger. By that time, three Sasquatches and two humans came flying around the corner. Gus and Joe had their rifles strapped to their backs and did not have a chance to unstrap them before the group was upon them.

I kept running as I heard the sounds of Gus and Joe being surrounded and captured. The last thing I heard was Gus swearing, then silence.

After about two miles, I was on a straightaway when I heard my chasers catching up again. My lead was down to 200 feet and two Sasquatches and Mike and Doug would catch me in moments. How on earth were those two humans running so fast, let alone those huge hairy beings!

I'd have to do something—and fast—if I was going to get away. With all my strength and willpower, I forced my body to speed up. I was running faster than any seven-mile race I had ever run, and they were still gaining! They had run three of the seven miles and my lead was down to fifty feet. The closest Sasquatch was just five feet behind me, and Mike and Doug were a few feet behind it.

No way around it, I would soon be a prisoner myself.

Unless...

As I went around the next bend, I took a sharp right turn into the thick wild blueberry bushes. I had often picked these wild berries as I walked through the small game trails that are about a foot wide and more like tunnels than trails.

Crashing through the bushes bent forward, I kept going at full speed. I had turned so quickly that the Sasquatch ran past where I got off the trail, and so did Mike and Doug. Because of their size, the Sasquatch wouldn't fit on these game trails. They'd have to run the road to follow me.

I was on a trail that went straight down the mountain to the river and came out not too far from our cable trolley. It was less than two miles down the trail, while it was four miles on the road.

Maybe I could still get away. There was no way the Sasquatch could keep up with me now. I was home free!

Then came the sounds of heavy running footsteps running the game trails behind me. Mike and Doug were following me! I could hear the sounds of branches and bushes breaking. It must be Mike who was wider than the narrow trails. Doug was faring no better. He was so tall he must have been scraping his back badly against the branches above.

It sounded as if Mike was on a trail to the right and Doug was on a trail to the left. But neither was gaining on me. I couldn't run very fast on the narrow trail, but all I cared about was being faster than the ones running behind me.

As I figured, the trail I was on came out 200 feet from the cable trolley. Doug and Mike were so far back I couldn't hear them. But where were the Sasquatch?

I sprinted to the trolley, jumped in, and quickly pulled myself across the river. On the other side, I jumped out and pulled the emergency cable release. The cable disconnected from the tripod and fell into the river. As the cable and trolley basket sank into the river, Mike and Doug came out of the bushes. Even from across the river, I could tell they were in rough shape. Both were bleeding from many small cuts. They caught sight of me across the river and sprinted towards me, yelling something. Not interested in having a conversation, I ducked down behind the cars while they ran to the river edge.

"Come out, we want to talk to you!" Doug yelled.

Peering over the car to see if there were any Sasquatch about, I saw the two men were not making an attempt to look for a way across. I walked to the river's edge, curious to know what they would say.

"We need help!" Doug yelled over the sounds of the river. "Is there any way you can help us escape?"

"No way, you tried to capture me. You're with the Sasquatch!"

"We had to make it look like we were trying . . . but all we want to do is escape."

No way I believed him after being chased like that. I was turning around to go to my van when Mike hollered, "Listen! Please!"

I turned and listened.

"We really want to get out. We can pay you if you come back and get us out."

"No," I said, shaking my head and turning to leave.

"Look out," Mike hollered. I turned all the way around in time to see Mike take his backpack off and throw it 100 feet across the river to near where I was standing.

The pack hit with a loud thud, raising a cloud of brown dust. Was it a trap? I approached the backpack warily and kicked the pack softly, and it felt heavy.

Mike yelled, "There's enough money in there to fund a big rescue."

Carefully, I opened the pack. Inside were a bunch of small bags the size of oranges. I pulled one out and opened it. The bag was heavy for its size, and when I opened it, it was obvious why. The bag was filled with gold coins. I pulled a couple more out and each also contained gold coins. At first look, the coins looked old and were in perfect shape.

Doug hollered out, "If you can find a way to meet back up the mountain where your camp is in three months, we will meet you there. We give you our word, we will escape and meet you there alone. Bring help to be safe."

I looked across at the men's faces. They appeared sincere.

Picking up the pack, I was astonished at its weight. It must have weighed at least fifty pounds. How could Mike have thrown fifty pounds a distance over 100 feet? And how could he have run so fast with it on?

There were so many questions I needed answered.

"OK, I'll try to get a rescue party there in exactly three months. But when I do, I'm going to bring an army to protect myself. I'm doing this for the guys who came with me. Those are the ones I want to rescue. Make sure they are with you."

"We will make it happen," Doug yelled.

"Wait," I said as a sudden thought hit my mind. "Doug, I'm sorry to tell you, but your mother...your mother passed away."

The tall man's shoulders slumped visibly, and he raised a hand partway up in acknowledgment before the two turned and started walking slowly back up the mountain.

I watched them go. Then I picked up the heavy pack and walked alone to my van.

ABOUT THE AUTHOR

Patrick Talmadge Sr. has always been a late bloomer. His growth didn't cease until he was over 21 years old. He reached his pinnacle as a national and world-class masters middle-distance runner at the age of 37, when he won his first master's national track and field championship in the 800-meter run.

At 47, Patrick earned his Bachelor of Arts degree and made history as the oldest NCAA cross-country runner. Seven years later, at 54, he returned to college to pursue a Master's degree in Psychology. During this time, he ran the mile in track, once again setting a record as the oldest NCAA track and field runner. He received his Master's degree in Psychology at 57. At the age of 66, he embarked on his writing journey.

Patrick taught himself to read at the tender age of three and a half and has been an avid reader ever since. With a keen interest in all fields of science, science fiction, and fantasy, he amassed a wealth of knowledge that would later prove invaluable when he began writing. Throughout his 20s and 30s, Patrick devoured two to three books a day. Upon graduating from graduate school in 2011, he retired from competitive running and felt a growing desire to write the stories that had been simmering within him.

In November 2021, spurred on by the love of his life, Patrick began his writing career. By July 2023, he had completed an adult four-book science fiction series about Sasquatch, a four-book children's series on the same subject, and a standalone novel about a senior community that befriends a troupe of Sasquatch.

Patrick possesses a unique ability to write multiple stories simultaneously, allowing him to modify and adjust interconnected narratives for clarity when writing a series. With a bit of luck, Patrick will continue to pursue his passion for writing for the rest of his life, or at least until his computer gives out.

ALSO BY PATRICK TALMADGE

Hidden Mountain Chronicles

Sasquatch Race

Sasquatch Prison Diary

Tenino Caverns

Sasquatch Home Planet

Sasquatch Chronicles

Hunter and Noah vs. Sasquatch Vol. 1

Hunter and Noah vs. Sasquatch Vol. 2

Hunter and Noah vs. Sasquatch Vol. 3

Hunter and Noah vs. Sasquatch Vol. 4

Sasquatch Senior Community Series

Sasquatch Senior Community

Sasquatch Senior Community: Lois and Mel the Beginning

Sasquatch Senior Community: The Early Years

Sasquatch Senior Community: The Middle Years

AFTERWORD

Go to hangar1publishing.com to learn more about the Authors and stay up to date with their newest releases.

www.ingramcontent.com/pod-product-compliance
Lightning Source LLC
Chambersburg PA
CBHW071158120626
46546CB00006B/2329